Mike Pearson was born in Darlington in 1956 and moved to York in 1969. Since 1978, he has lived in both the East and West Midlands where he has worked as a photographer and social worker before beginning to write, freelance, for music and literary reviews. He is married and has a daughter.

Mike Pearson

Northtown Exposure

Olympia Publishers
London

www.olympiapublishers.com
OLYMPIA PAPERBACK EDITION

ISBN: 978-1-84897-661-0

First published in 2016

Olympia Publishers
60 Cannon Street
London
EC4N 6NP
Printed in Great Britain

Dedication

To M, F and the Marstons

Acknowledgements

All photographs by Mike Pearson with grateful
acknowledgement to the football clubs of Darlington, York City
and Stafford Rangers.

'Little boys were locked out and old men lost their caps as
Darlington and Doncaster Rovers fought for the right to be
Fourth Division overlords.'
Bill Minns. Northern Echo 1968

'I think of your face among all those faces. Your hands tiny
in all that air applauding.'
Philip Larkin. Broadcast

CONTENTS

CHAPTER ONE
LINESMAN FOR THE COUNTY

A man waves to himself as he washes a window. Another face moves into view from the other side of the glass to blend with his. He sees that he's become someone else; an older woman indoors wearing a headscarf. He stops and pretends to rub her face. She calls him a daft beggar and tells him they'll want doing again.

'Who's that Eunice?' asks another woman's voice behind her.

'Only soft Dougie, he's about as much use with a shammy as he is training the first team.' She pauses and turns back into the room. 'Eee did you hear what happened last Saturday at Lincoln?'

'Is that Reenie?' he asks. 'Tell her I want her.'

'First them winders,' advises Eunice, then the two women fade away from his view through a connecting space into the grandstand's main corridor. They go into one of the smaller rooms laughing and close the door. In another room upstairs, with a long leather-topped table, hung several solemn oil paintings and stood by a sparse trophy cabinet, three men who were not laughing. They were trying to piece together a believable account of what happened to happen during a football match between Lincoln City and Northtown Athletic the previous weekend. The result was not the issue – a creditable draw away to the league leaders, which is a decent enough outcome but completely overshadowed by an off-the-field incident.

Mullins the manager sits ashen faced as Chairman Burleson shouts. 'You've turned this club into a laughing stock – what on Earth were you thinking man?'

The manager says nothing and lights up another plain cigarette with the stub end of his last one. The third man, younger and fitter looking, catches the manager's eye and clears his throat. 'From where I was on the pitch it looked a lot worse than it was, probably.'

The chairman cuts him short. 'If I thought it was that daft pillock's fault I'd have him in here, not you pair. No, as manager and club captain I expect you to give leadership. Incidentally Sproates, my wife could have put away that chance you missed, in her slippers.'

Captain Sproates says nothing and fixes his attention on one of the paintings. It is an improbable view of a stag at bay. The proud beast looks back at him as if to say, 'I wouldn't let him talk to me like that.'

Mr Burleson taps the table and speaks more gently. 'Well lads, come on, let's hear your side of things.'

Mr Mullins meets his chairman's eye and speaks. 'Well, obviously it was a mistake, it had been a cracking match and I decided we could snatch the winner and, well, it was a misunderstanding. I got a few men forward and signalled to Dougie to make sure the defence held. I called "Hold the line man!" Well, he clearly misheard me in the excitement of it all and…'

'Yes,' sighed Burleson. 'Peacock takes it into his head to embrace the linesman. I never knew he could move so gracefully – from where I was sitting it looked a complete farce. It might have been better if he'd roughed him up a little bit, but acting the giddy goat on the touchline! What did he think he was playing at?' He looked out of the window where a seagull flapped past. 'Lincoln's chairman sent me a copy of their "Green 'un" – here, make sure he sees it – the local Dispatch has already joined in. You know the linesman's called Fred? Well they've taken to calling Peacock "Ginger".'

Sproates tries to focus on the scenery and wonders if the picture is worth anything. Mullins opens the evening paper on the table and it's all there in black and green. The feature is titled 'Shall we dance?' and reference is made to 'coach Peacock's colourful display', 'unprecedented approach' and 'didn't know he cared'. There was also a large photograph of the brief melee following Dougie's intervention. There is a doughty constable wading in to restore order and make a point to Peacock and, on closer inspection, Mullins sees himself by the players' tunnel, just another face in the crowd. He also spots one of his own players – Hutchinson – laughing openly with two of their lads. Sproates asks his manager what Dougie was thinking. 'Goodness knows,' he replies. Burleson gets up and leaves the room without comment. 'I'll say one thing for him; he was right about that chance you missed' says Mullins, 'now nip off and see if Barry Hutch's about. Tell him to come and find me.'

Sproates heads for the treatment room where he makes himself comfortable on the phyiso's couch. He lights up an Embassy and hears a faint click, which wasn't his lighter. Deciding it was nothing he settles down for a closer reading of the sports paper for Saturday the fifteenth of March 1968, taking a special interest in the racing results. Further down the corridor Eunice and Reenie were washing footballs with abrasive powders. Outside Dougie finishes off the last of the windows and squeezes out his chamois cloth into a tin pail. They seem clean enough but he looks troubled and lifts his foot to kick the half-empty bucket over the fence. The dirty water goes all over the yard but it's still an impressive kick. 'Hey Dougie man yer've still got it – be back in the first team at this rate.' It's Guthrie, one of the nicer players, which at their level means least effective but Dougie knows he's a decent enough lad. He's glad it's him and not Hutchinson the cockney twerp forever taking the piss – biggest mistake Bob Mullins ever made taking him on, why did he think Brentford let him go for a brown envelope at Scotch Corner? Half the team wanted clearing out, he'd soon tell them, set of sand dancers. The first one to have a go and he'd swing for him.

'Aye, well, few more injuries and maybes I'll dust me boots down.'

'Just seen Skip down there on the table.'

'Eh? There's nowt wrong with him as far as I know.'

They go back into the back door of the stand. Dougie notices an odd feeling, that there is a third party somewhere, he was sure there was a figure hovering behind Ted Guthrie – a vague shape holding something in both hands, like a pigeon, lifting it for flight then melting away. He looks around but there's no one there.

It was something about the light through the fence setting up a loose rhythm as it picked out a stray football, a bucket on its side and the two men's heads from behind. He nearly caught it but the sun went in then the old bloke turned and almost saw him. Harold waited until the men had passed by and away down to the treatment room, then he slipped back into the car park.

He pulled an old butcher's bike free from some railings and pedalled off round the cricket ground adjoining the stadium.

Guthrie snatched the paper from Sproates and rolled it up to beat him about the head. 'Hey up Skip, what's this then a rest cure?' His teammate responded by twisting him onto the treatment couch and proposing a game of Emergency Ward Ten. Guthrie laughed and they wrestled like figures in a painting Barry Sproates was enormous, the biggest midfielder in the fourth division and, it was said, the daftest: but he was good. The wisdom of the wise in north-eastern sporting circles was that he had been good enough to make it at Middleborough but lacked the required 'edge'. Breaking Jackie Charlton's leg at Elland Road hadn't helped either and he was eventually offloaded to Northtown where he was made club captain. He loved being cock of the walk in this backwater and opposing defenders tended to remember his reckless challenge on Big Jack. They ended up in a genial roughhouse on the floor until Sproates accidently banged his pal's head against a pipe. Dougie closed the door on his way out. He knew that Ted had rolled up the paper to spare his feelings but wondered if he'd have been better off having a laugh. It was no good being nice in their game, had he thought Joe Royle was being nice when he'd punched the keeper in the kidneys in that cup game? We was robbed – we were mugged more like and sporting Ted had gone over to shake Royle's hand at the end like a bloody fool. They'd have had a laugh at that – Bally, Morrissey, right set of hard nuts. Time was there'd have been a good go afterwards in the tunnel. Football had gone soft. Dougie kicked a blameless chair, then marched off to the cricket club for a cup of tea.

'What was he after you for anyway?' said Eunice.

'Wanted to know if I'd seen his Robert last week. Someone had told him the lad had been across to see his auntie.'

'Robert still comes round to yours then?'

'Aye, won't speak to his father though and you can't tell Dougie.'

'Got a lot on his mind,' said Eunice. 'Probably what started that carry-on at Lincoln. They say the linesman was shaken.'

Reenie counted the balls and found there was one missing. Eunice thought it might be outside and went off to get it.

Some more players had turned up and were kicking the spare football around in the car park. Eunice stood watching with a hand on her hip like a fond aunt come to tell them to wash hands for dinner. She called that they needed the ball 'for testing' and a lad in winkle pickers rolled it across to her so well that she only had to bend without changing her stance. The ball had almost stopped moving by the time it got to her.

Graham was in the back kitchen looking at the hot water contraption above the sink.

'On the blink again?' said Harold.

'It was all right this morning when I made a coffee.'

'Straight from the tap?'

'Why not? Cools down quicker. It's your turn to phone the Little Waster and Shirley will be back next week.'

That decided it and they sat down on the stained deckchairs that served for a suite and chattered about Harold's pictures. The documentary aesthetic was given a good airing and he mused on the likely images he'd caught. 'There's a player smoking as he lay on a table reading the paper, couple of old dears nattering and one of the older guy they seem scared of remonstrating with someone. He seemed very upset but it's hard to know what's going on.'

Graham produced two pennies and the intrepid photographer went to phone the absentee landlord.

Back at the stadium training was being stepped up by the coach, Peacock, who had insisted on an extended session because he was in a bad mood. No one had objected. Manager Mullins and his chairman watched from the sidelines. 'It's odd them not ragging Doug,' said Mullins.

'Yes,' said Burleson. 'They don't generally need any encouragement for horseplay. It's like a storm brewing. Maybe Peacock would prefer it if one of them had a go, get it over with.'

Mullins cupped a hand to his mouth. 'Hey Dougie man, how about some formation dancing? That'd liven 'em up.' Cue massed laughter and a rueful grin from the coach.

Mullins led Tom off around the pitch to talk about a new player he had his eye on, a raw lad from West Auckland who might 'step up' to league level and 'put himself about' in the opposition's half. The chairman nodded without a firm enough grasp to ask too many questions. He knew he could trust Mr Mullins, they'd been lucky to get him. They looked back to the pitch where the players were doing a free-form maypole dance around a corner flag. Dougie was clapping his hands in time while Sproates conducted.

'Wish I had me camera,' said Tom. 'Hey, I knew there was something. We've been approached by Teesmade College of Art and Design, they want us to let a student document the club, be a fly on the wall, that sort of thing, during a season.'

'What did you say?'

'Told them to send him down with his camera for a chat – thought he might be here today. It could be good for the club.'

'Why not?' said Mullins. 'Can't do any harm.'

Back at Nixon Terrace Harold was sluicing some chemicals down the kitchen sink before the landlord, Mr Thompson called. As he poked at some congealed fried egg clogging the sink he became aware of a shape at the window in front of him. He looked up to see Mr Thompson standing patiently with the air of someone who'd been there a while. Before Harold could say anything he disappeared and came in through the back door.

'Now you said it wouldn't work.'

'Well no, it's just packed up, just comes through cold and nothing happens in the... doin's.'

Mr Thompson lit a cigarette and tapped a few pipes. 'It's knackered. What's that you're on with?'

Harold cleared his throat. 'I'm just developing some film actually – it's part of my course.'

'Oh aye, let's have a look then.'

'I'll need to pour out the fix and run some clear water through before we can see the negatives.' He moved towards the drain in the yard.

'Wouldn't it be easier to use the sink?' said Mr Thompson. 'I should think it's seen worse than lad's chemistry in its time.'

Harold tried to appear as capable as he could and attached a nozzle and short length of rubber to the tap and a fitting on his developing tank. He explained that the cold water would take ten minutes to run off the hyposulphites then they could examine the 'negs'. Mr Thompson did the clipped nod that seemed to say 'fair enough' in these parts and went for a sit down in the front room. Harold joined him. 'So you reckon the boiler's had it.'

'Done well to last this long by t'looks.'

Harold had no idea what his gnomic landlord intended to do about it and didn't know how to ask him. It was all right for some, he thought. He'd heard that Bobby Thompson lived in a big bungalow at Bishop Auckland, with a pig in the garden and central heating. 'I'd offer you a cup of tea but what with...'

'Aye, the boiler situation. Don't worry I've a pal in the trade, now what about these pictures?'

'Another couple of minutes. They're about the football club.'

'Is that what they teach you at college – how to waste film? Or maybe you could do a spot the spectator thing – then there's plenty of still life on the pitch. Aye, I can see it now.'

'They got a good result at the weekend.'

'Wasn't there some daft carryings-on with the linesman?'

'I don't know. Film should be ready by now.'

Mr Thompson watched Harold deftly handle two long rolls of film from the small tanks on to an improvised ledge hanging them clear of the window. He showed him how to hold the cellulite edges against the light so he could see what was there. Mr Thompson was interested and asked a couple of questions about lighting and lenses before giving off a sly chuckle. 'There's somebody here I know.'

He held the strip in a horizontal position. 'That one there, number twenty-eight is it?'

It was one of a series of the players mucking about in training. 'Do you know that player – I think he's called Thompson, is he a relative?'

'No, the man in the cap – Dougie Peacock. He's been around that club for years, used to play for them, wasn't bad as it happens but he's pulled a few stunts over the years, that one.'

'You watched him play for Northtown?'

'Yeah, they were crap then as well.'

Outside the steamy dressing room Tom Burleson smiled to himself as he caught the banter and slid a silver key into the door of his Singer saloon. He'd never played himself but he reckoned he understood footballers, their lives were like the army – they'd gripe and moan but they were decent enough lads who struggled if their lives weren't ordered for them. Local lads most of them, destined to pass through the club and on to nowhere in particular, but there'd be others just like them. He was aware of some changes recently, ringers from beyond the region, more rounded types like Barry Hutchinson from exotic Brentford who played the barrow boy but seemed a bit savvier, as he would no doubt put it. He'd taken Mrs Burleson to see him at the Lincoln game and she'd spotted the difference when he caught one of the Lincoln men with a sly rabbit punch. He hadn't liked what he'd seen either when Hutchinson went down like a bag of spanners after a tackle to win a free kick from a gullible official. Then laughing openly at Peacock's behaviour on the line. Too much success for the English game was spoiling it; now that Manchester United played sly South Americans on television, our lot were bound to be influenced by what they saw. Alf Ramsey had been quite right to criticise the rough stuff dished out by Argentina. He thought about the Lincoln match on his way home. What the devil had Peacock thought he was playing at? Hopefully it would all blow over with a good result against Hartlepool on Wednesday night. Hutchinson had better not try any of his London tricks then.

As he pulled away from Northfields Stadium Dougie twisted his way through one of the old rattley turnstiles to watch Burleson's big car on its way. Cunliffe, one of the younger players, approached him. 'Could you look at my leg please Mr Peacock? I think I've strained it.'

'Could you just pop off home and run yourself a hot bath son?'

'Oh, er right okay.'

'Sorry son – come in tomorrow and I'll have the physio sort you out.'

'Thanks Mr Peacock.'

Kenneth the grounds man had been listening and approached Dougie once the lad had limped off. 'Bit harsh on the kid Douglas.'

'Not you an' all – I've had it up to here with this club, should have stuck to selling pies on Stockton market.' He stalked back towards the club offices. Kenneth watched him go as he cranked up his line-marking machine.

The Burlesons lived in a large modern house on the smart side of town where the roads led to the pleasant Teesdale countryside. All built and paid for from the profits made by Burlesons Boilers, one of the town's more successful enterprises. Tom Burleson had taken his chances in 1962 when he'd remortgaged their previous place and won a government initiative grant. It was beginning to pay off and he was a significant employer of labour in the town, but his chairmanship of the Shunters let him in for unfair comment when the team did badly. After an especially poo show at Rochdale even Mrs Burleson was made to feel uncomfortable in the Walter Wilsons. He liked her to take an interest though, and she seemed keen to hear his thoughts on Dougie Peacock's antics when he got home.

'The papers'll make a meal of it won't they Tom?'

'I've already had a word with Newcombe at the *Scene*, he's sending a rookie reporter to get Dougie's version. Probably down there now.'

'So it should all blow over?'

'Yes, though a good showing on Wednesday would help. Has anyone phoned today?'

'No – were you expecting anyone?'

'Durkins from Doncaster, he reckons he's developed an exciting type of brass ring but he can't find the right fitting. We might be able to get in on it but it's all very hush-hush so he has to phone me here.'

Anita managed to contain her curiosity and said she'd put the kettle on if he wanted to go through. *Crossroads* was on.

'So when's his mate from Glow-Worm coming round?'

'I don't know and anyway it could be Warm-Glow, I can't remember now.'

Graham was looking at Harold's negatives. 'Worm-Glow? Did you know the chairman of your footer club owns a firm of boiler makers?'

'Oh, well I need to show him some of these.'

'Wouldn't you be better off showing him some prints?'

'I can't get into the dark rooms till next week.'

'Will he get us a television to go with the new boiler – Bobby Thompson I mean?'

'I didn't ask, we need the hot water on first – Shirl's back on Tuesday is it?'

'You'd best stick some Vim down the bog then – I'll hoover eh?'

'Listen Gray, there's a match on Wednesday night – fancy it?'

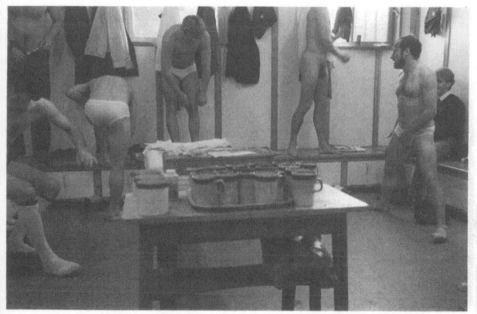

Dressing room before the game, York City, March 1983.

CHAPTER TWO

NORTHTOWN PEOPLE

Dougie free-wheeled down North Road past a sign for the general hospital, where a player from each side had spent time after last year's game with Hartlepool. He started pedaling again to pick up speed near the bottom and turned into Olympic Street.

'Awright Dougie?' Called a voice.

'Aye, not bad.' He replied warily, but the enquiry had been meant kindly and he recognised Mr. Suggett from number 9, who kept pigeons and a son with a motorbike. He liked them; Mrs. Suggett enjoyed singing at the social club on a Saturday and had been known to thump belligerent punters unmoved by her ballads and blues. Dougie admired her for that – people were too ready to mock these days. He pushed the bike along the side of his house and leaned it carefully against the wall, under the kitchen window. Inside, he removed his cap and clips then glanced up at a framed photograph in the hall. It was the late Mrs. Peacock who had been carried cruelly away by a road traffic accident ten seasons ago. He was about to tell her about his day when the phone rang. He hadn't been connected for long and still put on a formal voice. 'Northtown 3651, who is it please?'

'Is that you?' Asked the caller.

'Eh? Yes it's me - that's you then.'

'Yes Dougie, this is me, now we know who we are. Listen, I haven't got long, I'm supposed to be nipping out for some tabs so tell me what's going on.'

'Well we've got the big match this week and Sarah Suggett's...'

'Howay man, I'm not interested in that - I want to know how you are, you nearly caused a riot.'

Dougie sat on the stairs and sighed. 'Oh I don't know - Mullins shouted to hold the linesman, I could have sworn he did.'

'So you did.'

'Well I suppose I wasn't really thinking, it all happens so quickly during a match. No one got hurt. Can you get round later?'

'Not tonight pet, but you're all right though?'

'Yes just feel a proper Charlie.'

'Right, well listen carefully, after the big match eh? I'll phone you later on, could you get home by 10?'

'I'll try - phone anyway.'

'Right, bye then.'

'Aye.'

He replaced the receiver and turned away from the woman on the wall to fetch an old rug sweeper from under the stairs. Dougie then spent the next hour doing the place from top to bottom, before rewarding himself with a round of ham sandwiches in the kitchen. His mood eased after the vigorous housework and he switched on the portable set he kept by the bread bin. There was a play on about a man called Latimer, who was being grabbed by the lapels as another man asked him what the hell he knew about Laura. He consulted his Radio Times; Tuesday Night Rep was presenting 'The Snake Is Living Yet', where a woman goes to Tangier to escape a broken marriage but finds herself at the heart of a mystery that ends with violence and death. Dougie listened as the drama played itself out and went to bed in a reflective mood.

Across town at the Cats Whiskers Club, Barry Hutchinson was moving in on the week's conquest, using his athletes body smoothly as she and her mate hopped a polite bop to Gary Pucket and the Union Gap. He joined them and asked if this was the way up the junction.

'You're not from round here like.' She said.

'You aint wrong there like.' He replied.

His 'mate' Guthrie, fretted at the bar and felt he ought to get the cockney chancer home soon.

'Her mate fancies you.' Said Hutchinson.

'Sod that, I'm off home.' Said Guthrie.

'Oh well, suit yourself.' Said Hutchinson and sashayed his way back to the dance floor, as Matt Monroe oozed from some state of the art Bang and Olafsen speakers. "Born free to follow your heart" he crooned and handed her a Babycham, when they sat down together. Guthrie walked home alone wondering if Northtown was ready for footballers like Barry Hutchinson.

'What do you reckon to this London lad they've signed up, Kenny ?' Said Eunice.

Kenneth was busy dabbing one of the penalty spots with white lime. 'Hutchinson? His nearest neighbour in the team is Smithy from Stoke and he cracks on to be this leagues Rodney Marsh.'

Eunice let out a wheeze. 'They've not put Smudger in for tonight? They'll draw him out of position then do us down the left. Mullins wants looking at if you ask me - fancy playing that carthorse.'

'No not Smith - Hutchinson fancies himself, reckons it's funny for Guthrie to call him Romney Marsh - and you can tell Bob wouldn't have thought that one up for himself. Anyway, Dougie tells me Smithy's knackered again so Bob's putting in the young 'un from Billingham.' Eunice was concerned about a youth being bloodied against the Poolies, but Kenneth was able to reassure her. 'He'll be alright; Big Bill'll keep an eye on him.' She shuffled off to meet Reenie and see to the pies, while Kenneth had a last look at his markings. A heavy rain during the afternoon had left the playing surface thick and slippery; perfect conditions for the defense to put the skids under Tommy Hancock, Pools danger man, the best prospect they'd had since Amby Foggarty and, it was said, being closely watched by several of the big teams. Don Revie had been spotted in Stockton High Street, but Reenie said he was just on the way to visit his Mother. Anyway, thought Kenneth, if they could contain in nippy Hancock they might stand a chance. He gathered up his bucket and brush to store them back under the smaller grandstand. It was six-thirty and the place was deserted. Apart from a cluster of round lights over by the player's tunnel there were no intimations of the titanic encounter to come. Kenneth took a much delayed piss by a large poplar and went off for his tea to the grace and favour maisonette by the cricket scoreboard, where Dougie generally called in for a natter before an evening game.

Across in the dressing rooms most of the players were present and the early doors banter was giving way to serious stuff as the kick off drew closer. 'She had tits out here.' Confided

Hutchinson, cupping his hands like a giant about to wash his face.

'Oh aye.' Said Thompson. 'Seeing her again then?'

'Said she'd be there tonight - fancy coming?'

'Nah, told our lass I'd be round at her Mothers to collect her by ten.'

'Bring 'em both along then.'

Thompson couldn't help laughing. 'You cheeky beggar - Christ, see her Mother in a nightclub.'

Someone else chimed in about seeing Big Bill's Mother in a nightie and the idea took off. Stanton, the midfield 'terrier' wondered aloud how the chairman's wife might fill a negligee. It was agreed that Anita Burleson was a very handsome woman 'for her age like' and would do very nicely in any nightwear she cared to put on. Then manager Mullins came in and Guthrie roused the troops. 'Right lads, big night tonight, are they in next door yet boss?'

'Yes, I've just had a cup of tea with boss Williams, he told me they're resting Hancocks and lining up with two wingers. He must think I'm crackers if he expects me to believe that. Kick 'im first chance you get Bill.'

'Will do boss.'

Mullins looked around the room carefully. 'Where's Dougie?'

'Dunno Boss,' said Sproates. 'Maybe 'Come Dancing' is on tonight.'

Mullins smiled and winked at the young lad from Billingham, who'd been sitting quietly taking it all in. 'It's better than the London Palladium at this club son, eh Hutch.'

Hutchinson answered in overblown geordiese, then Dougie appeared before Mullins could bollock the silver-tongued schemer. Nobody else spoke and the focus switched to tactics and set pieces, where Dougie argued for an element of surprise involving 'the kid'.

At Nixon Terrace the gasman had come to call and the news was bad. 'Mr. Thompson said we'd need a new one putting in,' said Harold.

'Aye well he was right enough there.' Said the man, as he peered at the exposed workings and whistled softly. Harold was getting a bit fed up with the strange ways of the quirky locals, were they taking the Mick, or what?

'Well, what do you think?'

'What I think is it needs looking at.'

Harold left him to it and went to talk to Graham, who asked him what he'd said.

'Not much, reckons it needs seeing to. I thought that was why he was here?'

Graham put down his sketchpad. 'Are we off then?'

Before Harold could reply intelligence came from behind the door. 'It'll all need ripping out, complete refit - ought by rights to be declared unsafe, no-one's to touch it - Burleson's top man needs to see this. You don't find many like this these days, whole street could have gone.'

'I think I preferred him as the quiet man.' Muttered Harold as he opened the door.

'I'm sealing it off - no naked lights. I'll report to Thompson tomorrow, off to the match?'

'Yes, yes we are actually.' Said Graham.

'Well keep an eye on Guthrie, he's Burleson's top man - if he comes through unscathed we've room for hope. He's the only fitter in this town fit for a job like this.' Then he packed his tools into a thin canvas bag and left.

'What an odd chap.' Said Graham.

'Too much gas.' Said Harold and went to fetch his camera.

Graham went out into the back lane to wait for his mate where he met Ambrose coming back from walking his Mothers dog. The animal was a rheumy-eyed neurotic with the body of a spaniel and the head of Alfredo Garcia. Shirley had dubbed her 'Glaxo' given that only a brief encounter between a bull terrier and a chemical works could have conceived her. She actually answered to Pansy and was shaping up to mucky the cobbles when Ambrose pulled her in and favoured Graham with a fierce nod. He wished Harold had been there with his camera but Harold had been delaying his entry until Ambrose banged the back door. 'We'd best look sharp.' He said. 'There'll be a big gate tonight.'

Graham had only a rough idea what Harold meant, but guessed it was footballers banter.

'Right lads,' said Mullins and clapped his hands. 'Half hour to kick-off, me and young Douglas are off to see the chairman for a word or two. Should be about ten minutes then we'll work out how to sink the 'Poolies - from a cunning corner kick, eh Dougie.' He closed the door behind him; one of the players lit up a cigarette.

Sproates pulled a rueful face. 'If it's anything like it was up at their place we've no chance. Everytime we got the ball up into their box Billy Hampson kicked lumps out of us -ref was having none of it, if he's playing tonight I'm gonna do him, whatever Professor Peacocks cooked up it's lights out for Hampson.'

'What do you reckon Dougie's on about?' Asked Borthwick, one of the wide men who usually took corners.

'Who knows,' said his skipper. 'Formation dancing if he's in charge.'

This got a tense laugh and the mood was becoming more focused. Thompson asked Sproates what he thought had got into Dougie Peacock lately. 'Who knows?' He answered levelly. 'He's not been right for months, it's maybes time they give 'im the bullet.'

'Not Dougie, surely not, he's the heart and soul of this club. Imagine Northtown Athletic without Dougie Peacock.'

'You're too soft you are,' chided Sproates. 'We're none of us indispensable; Dougie'll have to sort out his own problems. Now you concentrate on Tommy Hancock.'

Up in the boardroom chairman Burleson and his charming wife were entertaining a group of dignitaries from Hartlepool. The visiting chairman, a misanthropic car dealer called Willis, was holding forth on gearboxes. Mullins and Dougie let themselves in.

'Ah here they are now.' Said Burleson in his best form master with unpromising boys voice and Anita stepped forward to offer sherry, apologising to Dougie for there being no beer.

'Sherry'll do very nicely Mrs. Burleson.' Said Mullins.

'Oh, Anita please Bob - we're all friends here. You too Doug.'

Willis looked up smartly at mention of Dougie's name but soon returned to the quixotic nature of the motor trade. After a few words with the rest of the visiting directors, one of whom wore a monocle, manager and coach left for more important business. 'Come on then Doug let's get our lot fired up. You can bet Dick Willis has his lot on a bonus for tonight.' Dougie nodded as he savoured the sweet aftertaste of boardroom sherry.

Kenneth was lending a hand with the extra turnstile; put on to cater for 'the vast amount of folk' forecast for the match by the Northern Scene. He'd been very busy taking the three shillings admission but still noted the two young men with the camera and had a few words with them. 'What was he on about?' Asked Graham as they filed round the cricket field.

'I dunno, seemed friendly enough like.' Graham gave Harold another puzzled glance then asked if he'd be able to use the flashgun. 'No, but I'm going to up rate the film and develop it in college next week.'

The compact stadium didn't need many spectators to give it an atmosphere, especially for an evening game. There were 5000 or so there already and with the floodlights on the spectacle made Graham gasp. Everybody seemed to know what they were doing and where to stand. Over someone's shoulders he could see a small hut where two ladies were dishing out steaming pies. He expected one of them to push a hole in the middle of the pies to blob gravy in. It was like a scene from a Dutch fairy tale or a rose tinted cameo of Northern life - he felt like a ruddy cheeked bairn off to see the fair. Then the man in front let off a cavernous fart and his mate breathed beer as he laughed. Graham nudged Harold over to the side of their queue and asked him where they should stand. 'Behind the goal.' He said decisively.

Over the tannoy - sponsored by Yourbeat records - Crosby Stills and Nash were aboard the Marrakesh Express. 'Fookin 'ippy shite.' Said an adjacent youth and glared at Graham.

Elsewhere Mullins was weaving his pre-match magic. 'Take no prisoners lads and hit them before they hit you.'

'What's this corner kick routine boss?' Asked Borthwick.

'Dougie will explain.'

All eyes turned to him. This was his chance to win back a little respect, come through with the kind of hard won wisdom that had served them so well in the past. 'Well,' he said. 'It's not very complicated, it's really just a decoy to draw them out of position and open up space in front of their goal with the sudden element of surprise.'

'Aye.' Said Sproates. 'But how do we work the thing, we don't want any nasty surprises.'

'Right, well supposing Borthy goes in to take a corner, young Atkinson should run towards him shaping up to receive the ball short but a third man - doesn't matter who, decide between yourselves - lurks behind the lad and takes the ball instead. Atkinson's marker is wrong footed and we get some time and space to get the ball into the box.'

'We can only do it once though can't we?' Reasoned Fiddler the other winger.

Dougie had anticipated this. 'Well they won't know if we'll do it more than once so it gives them more to worry about. The element of surprise you see.'

As the players jogged out Sproates turned to Thompson. 'Well you can't say Dougie isn't a surprising man can you.'

'Do you reckon it'll work Skip?'

'We'll see but I'm keener on surprising Hampson, if you can fettle Hancock as well we'll consider it a good nights work.'

The Hartlepool players had come out before the home side and were warming up in front of the goal where Harold and Graham were standing. Trilby the 'Pools goalie was enormous and looked capable of stopping any shot with one hand, and some of the other players were so stocky they seemed to lack knees. Their thighs just seemed to taper a bit towards their feet. Graham felt out of his depth. The painting school on his fine art course hadn't prepared him for vernacular culture at such close quarters. Many of the men appeared drunk and there were women present, shouting. He knew that Caravaggio had had his moments but had Gwen John ever been to the bingo?

Above the rabble in the executive section of the grandstand the special party unscrewed their hip flasks and discussed the young prospect Mullins had picked for the big game. 'He certainly likes to surprise, your manager.' Said Willis.

'Oh I think you'll see a few surprises tonight.' Said Burleson. His wife looked straight ahead watching the poplars above the stand sway like weeds under water. 'Yes,' went on Tom, 'we've high hopes for the lad. Newcastle were after him as a youth teamer but once Peacock had met the family and had a word he agreed to come here. He's an excellent man Peacock, first class.' Anita looked to the trees and the match got underway. Hartlepool had won the toss and elected to play towards the home end where the two aesthetes were trying to enjoy themselves.

'Have you taken any pictures yet?'

'Yeah, got a few of the crowd around us - I'm just off to the back of the terracing to see how much of the pitch I can get. Be back in a bit.' Then Hartlepool scored. All Graham knew about it was a sudden concentration of activity on the right hand side of the pitch, several players running towards the goal then a slow motion roar from the other end of the ground as Northtowns goalie picked himself up and scooped the ball out of his net. It had all seemed to happen out of nothing, but several white shirted players stood with their hands on their hips, as a gaggle of blue shirts ran to their fans waiving.

The crowds good spirits began to turn; 'should have closed him down' - 'Thommo's past it' - 'shite man'. It took a turn for the worse ten minutes later when Hartlepool scored again. Thompson was involved, getting into a muddle with another white shirt and giving the ball away just outside the penalty area. The Hartlepool player seemed to know exactly where the ball was going and kicked a fantastic shot straight past the goalie. Even Graham could see it had been well done but the home supporters were incensed, at least one pissed bloke looked ready to mount the waist high barrier to make this point to the goalkeeper, but a young policeman showed his face. 'That's Hancocks second, he'll beat us on his own the way bloody Thompsons playing.' Moaned a figure to Graham's right. He wished Harold would come back, he could speak the language.

Things settled down a bit after this. The blue players seemed content to stay down the other end and let the white shirts have more of the ball. A shot from a Northtown man went close and the crowd began to get behind them again, then there was a prolonged hold-up while one of the blue men was helped to limp off the pitch by the player, Graham now knew to be Thompson and the Hartlepool trainer who then tried to thump Thompson, who as far as Graham could see was only trying to help. There was a great bally-hoo from the crowd as another Hartlepool player confronted Thompson and the referee intervened. After some more shoving and waving of fists Thompson was booked and Hartlepool awarded a free kick. Graham's new friend leaned over. 'I'll say this for Bill, he can still kick another player sweetly enough.' Graham edged away from him over to the other side of the goal to stand near two head-scarved women who were agreeing that it had been about time for Thompson to do something right. He decided to concentrate on the action and learn what he could. Most of it was happening at the other end and another Northtown effort was pushed over the bar by the bulky but agile Trilby. Corner to Northtown. A white shirt trotted over and placed the ball ready to belt it into the goalmouth. It all seemed straightforward until he turned at the last minute and passed it short to another white shirt, who looked about 13 years old to Graham. He let it run through his legs to another team mate who moved forward with the ball and chipped it delicately across the penalty box where it was headed neatly past a puzzled Trilby. Graham was buoyed along by the fantastic cheering and hoped there'd be more goals to come. He began to wonder how he might get some of this into a painting.

It wasn't long after this that the whistle went for half time and the players were clapped off. As the tannoy played '*Poetry In Motion*' Graham shuffled through the mass to the spot where Harold had left him. He found him faffing about with his camera and some film. 'Well, what did you make of that?' He said.

Graham thought for a while. 'Did you ever read that account of the first night of 'The Rite of Spring'?'

'No... I don't think I ever have. Not in the local paper anyway, why?'

'Well the crowd was probably a bit like that and if you could have got Duchamp to paint some of the action...'

A third party behind them interrupted the brains trust. 'Oo the fuck's ee- bringing 'im on for t'second 'alf or what?' Stale ale reinforced the belligerent air of a man who knew a tosser when he heard one, even if he had only a vague grasp of modern painters.

'Fancy a Bovril?' Said Harold and directed them away from the fan who was saying something to his mate and glaring at them. He had second thoughts about some candids of the crowd in the second half. They managed to get lost in the throng and were forced towards the crush barrier separating them from the pitch at ground level.

'Actually I'm not bothered about that Bovril,' said Graham. It had become quite difficult to move, as the crowd behind them began to thicken and the home fans made for the area their team would be attacking in the second half. He could feel people behind them and sensed a great barely contained weight. Cigarette smoke, wet grass and the smell of male farts gave the night a scent of menace. Further back, a massed choir from hell were singing a song about the Hartlepool manager and a monkey. There were so many people pressed about him that he could hardly turn. Harold had his camera out and seemed keen on catching a man near the corner flag throwing twisted paper bags of peanuts high into the crowd, people were throwing coins back to him. Silver sixpences on the grass were floodlit night flowers. If any bags fell short someone would pick them up and lob them back to the punters behind. He had another idea for a painting. The peanut vendor came closer and Harold became very excited, as he was able to catch him close up. Graham could see the grace and subtlety of it in amongst the swearing and brutality, just like the football. From the talk around him he'd gathered that the injured player had been 'knobbled' and would be unable to continue. Even he'd worked out that Hancock was Hartlepool's best player and given them an edge.

Harold was still straining after the man with the basket and was sitting astride the barrier to get more room. He leaned over a bit more then someone pushed him all the way over onto the pitch. 'There yare mate, you can get a close up of his arse now.'

Harold had fallen on his side and was wheezing. 'Hey!' Shouted Graham, 'leave him alone.'

'Ooo there's another one here,' said someone. 'Let's make a bit of space eh - after you Claud.' Then Graham felt himself borne across the barrier by several strong arms and placed roughly beside Harold who was now on his knees and rubbing mud from his lens. The young policeman watched what was happening but stayed where he was. Harold led them off towards the goal where a press photographer sat on his metal box. Harold explained that they were from 'The Sunday Times Magazine' and asked if they could sit with him. After some reporters' chat about film speed and rates of pay he spread out some canvas for them and Graham was invited to sit down, to get his impressions for the story he would write to accompany Harolds pictures. Then the teams came out together for the second half. The noise behind them was frightening; Graham wondered how the players could concentrate.

Once the game got going again it was clear that Northtown was making a special effort. Every tackle and pass was cheered, from their new position Graham could see how quickly things happened, how much movement went on even when a player didn't have the ball at his feet. How rough it was as well; two men charged into each other going after the ball and the impact took them both off their feet. One of them crashed against the barrier and his opponent helped him up then they hared off back into the fray, where a blue shirted player smacked the ball against the bar. The ball was lofted back towards their end for a white shirt, who shielded it and seemed to be heading away from the goal only to squeeze it between a blokes legs from behind and turn back bypassing another Hartlepool defender. He was suddenly free inside the penalty box and thumped the ball past Trilby to level the score. Graham jumped up and shouted. Harold was focusing on the crowd taking pictures quickly as they leaped and bawled behind the goal.

Across at the dugouts Dougie had taken on a peacekeeping role as Mr. Mullins and the opposing bench begged to differ over the finer points of Hancocks injury, it now being clear that he would be spending the night in hospital. A suggestion had been put forward that his manager might care to join him there and the disagreement threatened to worsen. Dougie managed to bring harmony where there had been discord and wandered past the ball boy to look up to the executive box. He saw Burleson's big face turn to say something and a smaller hand hover briefly to the chairman's left. 'Hey Dougie man you've got 'em geed up champion for this.' Called a friendly voice. He thought that if they could turn this round tonight everybody could start looking forward.

Harold had come over to Grahams side of the goal and was now talking to the press guy about the problems of getting pictures printed to the best standard. He couldn't help admiring his mates brazen claims - maybe it could come true. 'Aye,' agreed his new friend. 'You go to all this trouble then the editor sits on it.'

The game seemed to Graham to have gone off the boil a bit, with both teams struggling to get near each other's goal. He asked Harold how much longer there was to go. He told him about ten minutes then the press bloke, Ernest, directed their attention to the dugout where Mullins was talking urgently to the substitute, while Dougie signaled furiously to one of the men on the pitch who trudged off and sat down. The fresh player ran on to a cheer and took more instructions from Sproates. Play resumed with a free kick and Ernest pointed out that the new man had taken up a defensive role to enable the 'young 'un' to go forward and use his pace. As far as Graham could see it made no difference; the ball still seemed to spend more time in Northtowns defense than anywhere else. Then Northtowns goalie belted the ball right up field for the guy who had scored the second goal, to control it deftly with his chest and roll it delicately between two blue shirts for the young player to run on to. The crowd responded and Graham felt the sudden thrill as he dashed towards the Hartlepool goal area. There was one more player in his way but he took the ball round him with an exquisite shimmy and looked set to shoot when the defender tripped him clumsily from behind. The place erupted with a collective affront as the offender - 'dirty Hampson - send the booger off - it's a penalty man' - stood with his hands up. Both the Sunday Times boys were fascinated by the theatre of it all; the young lad was enraged and had to be restrained from hitting the older man, a seasoned old pro, who could have been his uncle, who then managed to claim some moral credit by making no bones about bringing him down. The ref sent him off just the same to cheers and mockery and the ball was placed on the penalty spot, so carefully marked out by Kenneth earlier. The skilful player who'd made the chance lined up to take it - 'howay Hutch, put it away man' someone bawled. The player grinned and waved to the crowd who seemed to like his nerve. The goalkeeper danced on the line like a boxer and Hutchinson ran at the ball. He smacked it incredibly hard to the goalie's left but he made a tremendous leap to push the ball against the post. The power of the shot meant that he couldn't catch it and the ball pinged across the goal area and the player who'd been fouled dived to head it into the net just ahead of a defender who was stretching to kick the ball clear but caught him on the shoulder instead. Every base emotion known to even a halfway sentient soccer fan fizzed into life as the place went bonkers. As far as Graham could see it had been an accident, but a free form wrestling bout had begun in the goalmouth as the plucky lad was helped to his feet and some of the crowd pushed towards the barriers shouting encouragement. Then things settled down a bit and the game resumed with Northtown in the lead. There was a brief scare when Hartlepool hit the bar again but the home side held on, and after the final whistle the players shook hands before walking off to generous applause.

Ernest held his esteemed colleagues back for a while, then advised them to go with him round the edge of the pitch to the tunnel where people were milling and one of the players was chatting with a linesman. Harold was tempted to produce his camera again but thought better of this; plenty of time, but tonight had been a good start. He couldn't wait to develop the film. He was taking it all in for future reference then changed his mind when he noticed how the wooden huts by the pitch seemed to behead anyone standing behind them. Then he noticed that one of the figures was staring back at him. It was the man he'd spotted before who seemed to be about a lot. 'Alright kidder.' He called across gruffly. 'Candid Camera is it?'

'It's alright Doug,' said Ernest. 'These young men are from the Sunday Times Magazine.'

'You what - this clubs in the Times?' Dougie was alarmed now and was keen to learn more when a gentle hand on his shoulder drew his attention and Ernest nudged his charges forward. 'Right, straight through with me and out the back door - no hanging about.' Harold caught a glimpse of a Hartlepool player being held up against a dressing room wall by a man in an overcoat and wondered if he'd be able to get any pictures like that. Outside Ernest gave them his card and a firm invitation to call him at the Scene as it wasn't often that the nationals took an interest in Northtown. Harold felt a prat and was glad when they went their separate ways.

Dougie had forgotten about the two weirdo's Ernie Todd had in tow and was talking to Mullins as the players showered. The

45

manager was feeling pretty good. 'Well Douglas we steadied the ship and caught the wind.'

'Pushing the kid up made the difference.'

'Yes, you've done a good job with him - showed his mettle when that clot Hampson kicked him. Hey see the way Big Bill clattered Hancock, he's crap with the ball but you tell him which player to knobble and he's a world-beater.'

'A panel beater more like.' Said Dougie, who didn't like to see players injured like that.

'You can't be a purist at this level ...'

'Aye well. Listen, do you mind if I get off early?'

'No of course not and thanks for tonight, I reckon we can develop that corner kick excuse me, eh?'

Dougie passed through the stragglers hanging around in the corridor and found the Hartlepool manager to ask after Hancock. They agreed it was a bad business and that Big Bill had better not stray north of Shildon for the time being. Hancock would be all right and Dougie promised to have a word, then he threaded his way across the cricket field to his bicycle. Someone had pinched his dynamo but he took his chances through the back streets to get home by half-nine. The phone went at ten to. 'Is that you pet?' He asked directly.

'What if it wasn't?'

'Eh? Oh I knew it would be you - can you get?'

'Yes, they'll be on over here for a while yet - an hour maybes.'

'Well park up the road and come round the back.'

'Don't worry.'

He put the phone down and glanced guiltily at the photograph, then he went into the front room to plump his cushions. Ten minutes later the back door echoed a polite tap. Dougie opened the door and asked. 'Is that you pet?'

She came in and looked around the kitchen. 'Make us a cup of tea Doug, I've had enough sweet sherry for one night. Can I…?'

'Yeah, you know where it is.'

He got organised as quickly as he could and wiped down his hostess trolley as the sex-rinsed scent of fresh cigarette smoke drifted through to him. 'Good game tonight.' She said as he fussed with the trolley.

'Mmm - good result anyhow.'

'It looked very eventful from where I was sitting.'

'It's not the way I like to see football played. That carthorse Thompson could have ruined their lads career - there was a scout there from West Brom you know.'

'Oh the accident, their chairman was very angry about it all.'

'Well he would be, his prize asset crippled by a half-baked brickie from Ferryhill. He'll be all right mind, I spoke to their boss - hey, something else, I had a word with Ernie Todd too. He had a right pair of scruffy beggars with him, from the Sunday Times Magazine.'

Anita sucked on her cigarette with a faraway look, then tapped it delicately into the tin ashtray Dougie kept for special guests. He watched her openly, enjoying the poise and knowingness she managed to give off. Watching her smoke a cigarette at last years reserve match with Northallerton had been what finally did it for him. 'We'd better be careful then.' She said.

'Eh?'

'Sunday Times - don't want it in the papers.'

'Don't read it meself.'

'Neither do we. Tom swears by the Express - I get half an hour with it before I've to get his roast on.'

Dougie never felt comfortable discussing Mr. Burleson in this setting. Anita usually knew to keep him out of things, perhaps they'd had words at the match. He clapped his hands decisively. 'Shall we dance pet?'

'That would be nice.' She said and stood up. She was wearing pearls and her full figure seemed to shimmer before him. He anticipated the joys of her bosomy embrace as he turned to select his Artie Shaw long player. When the music began she held her arms open and they came together to move about the room to the heady rapture of 'Moonglow'. 'You're a lovely mover.' She said and kissed his neck.

'How long have we got?' He asked and stroked her bottom. She didn't answer but when 'Begin the Beguine' began she steered him into the hall.

CHAPTER THREE

HOT WATER

'What time did Shirl say she'd be back, Gray?'

'Dunno. You off in this morning?'

'Yeah – I want to get last night's done.'

'Right, well, let's get the place smartened up then,' said Graham. Harold gave back a firm nod and went about collecting stray crockery and odd rubbish. Graham heaved the furniture around and within ten minutes their little bower had regained its ideal of shabby welcome. Harold piled pots into the sink and Graham said he'd do the bathroom later. 'What about the little boiler?' he asked.

'Oh, that bloke was supposed to be doing something about it,' said Harold as he went out of the house. Graham fetched the Vim.

The College was sited in an older part of the town at a former school near a leafy park. Harold soon joined several cyclists heading in the general direction, many of them were from a nearby factory going in for the later shift. He smiled benignly at the artisans and looked forward to the day when every works would have its own exhibition venue and the fitters could read Colin Wilson in their tea break. He left his bike behind an annex and made for the school of printing.

'A few in for treatment this morning Bob.' Mullins and Burleson were standing behind one of the goals, milking what was left of the post-match euphoria. The manager looked out across the pitch. 'Always a tough game with them, nearly came to blows with Boss Williams myself as a matter of fact. The kid took a knock for his troubles.'

'Didn't he put it away well though? We must get him on a proper contract Bob, as Hancocks won't be moving for a while they'll all be running the rule over young Atkinson now.'

Mullins smiled to himself. 'He did well enough but it's early days yet – best keep his feet on the deck. Seen this mornings paper?'

'Not yet, good write-up?'

'Not bad.' He pulled a copy of *Northern Scene* from his overcoat to read some selected extracts. 'Until Thompson's meaty challenge it had been Hancock's half-hour with the visitors rampant... Hutchinson's guile picked the lock... manager's crafty switcheroo... young man with a future... Hampson's disgrace.'

'Yes,' said the chairman emphatically. 'Just so, the man's no better than a thug. What do they mean by *switcheroo*, I thought you made a substitution?'

'It was, they've got a comedian from somewhere covering us this year. I think it's an American expression.'

'Like rain check?'

'Probably.'

'No mention of unorthodox behaviour on the sidelines?'

'Not that I could see and I read the thing twice. Now, what about this photographer?'

'Eh? Oh, I'm sure it'll be all right, I think Peacock can take him under his wing, keep him out of trouble. Which reminds me that blooming case should be coming up with the FA – I need to have a word with the Lincoln chairman, there must be something we can do. He's a good man, grows potatoes.' Mullins watched his chairman walk over to the club offices and wondered if Dougie had his chips from their chairman's table, too.

The visiting photographer was telling the group how freelancing in America had helped him to see how much work there was to be done in England. How, apart from 'Bill Brandt and one or two others', nobody had 'stepped like Alice through the looking glass' to discover how the world could look. How the English in their quirky understated way were ripe for a creative harvest. Photographers with their cameras could aspire to what Orwell had done with his typewriter. Harold found it all very exciting and when they got the chance to see some of the chap's work – taken around the country on his travels in a camper van – he felt both a thrill of recognition and a dull sense of failure. He knew what this photographer was on about and could see it in his pictures, but he couldn't see himself producing stuff that good. In his talk Phillips had referred crushingly to good intentions being not enough and something about getting in close to the subject but staying remote enough to get some composition – 'pictures fall apart without it'.

Quite a few of his pictures had been taken at the seaside and the more Harold looked at them the better they seemed. The way he'd laid out the objects and people in the frame was wonderfully poised. The human shapes were the main thing. Even when they were overlooked by sky or concrete and metal they gave off a tough warmth and dignity. In one study, taken the previous summer at a beach in the south he'd managed to still a random group of people around some boys playing cricket in a sort of dance which filled the entire frame. People rarely looked so free or graceful in real life but this was real; for one hundred and twenty fifth of a second it had been and here was the proof. He'd seen it and now Harold could. He'd sensed that this guy was hard-boiled and shrewd – wouldn't use phrases like 'the redemptive power of photography' but he obviously had it. He'd also stressed that it was important to have a feeling for your subject and that a photographer's integrity should show in their pictures. Again, he could see it this guy's pictures, but what about his own?

Harold resolved to get back down to the club that afternoon and get his sleeves rolled up. He left his films with his tutor who agreed to put them through with some other stuff and do him a contact sheet of all the negatives. Terry said it sounded 'potentially very interesting' adding that if Tony Phillips was still around he'd ask him to have a look. Harold found his bike and got on it, as he took off down the road he reflected that everything was potentially interesting.

Tom Burleson paused outside his kitchen window to see inside. Then he stood up and marched round to the back door whistling audibly. 'Hello dear, thought I'd look in first thing, have a few words with Mullins. I bumped into Peacock on the way, he was singing to himself – something about begonias. He's always seemed such a dour man, must have been last night's result. That's something else, I must give Willis a ring is that tea still warm?'

Mrs Burleson made an obvious effort to concentrate on the paper as he shuffled around their capacious kitchen prattling to himself, then out into the hall to call his awful pal. She read on and tried to absorb some stuff about the effects of devaluation on small businesses. Elsewhere Mr Heath had promised to make the trains run on time if the travelling public ever gave him the chance and concern had been felt locally about sheep rustling at Richmond. 'I say Anita, it's all right for them to come over for a spot of supper next week?' he called with his hand not over the receiver.

'Yes that would be very nice,' she trilled, thinking that an evening with that interbred hooligan and his doxy was more than she could stand, having had enough of her last night with her fish face, lazy eye and interest in dancing linesmen. There was more banter from 'Tommy' over the phone then he took himself off upstairs. She felt rotten, none of this was right – if she'd any guts she'd pack it in and settle for what she'd got.

Better than risking the lot.

Harold called in at home for his camera and some film. There was no one there. He avoided the kitchen but the old lady from next door caught him out the front to let him know that Mr Thompson had been 'about the gas' and would call later. He told her not to worry but that he had to 'nip somewhere' and would be back later as well. 'Ambrose thought he could smell something!' she called after him. *Probably you* he thought and sped away in case her doting son was about. When he reached the ground he was more wound up but determined to get in closer to a subject he had feelings about. It was what he sometimes called 'the poetry of the everyday' or, if he felt his audience merited it, 'the quotidian'; anyway he'd always loved football. That was all you needed.

He spotted a couple of men pulling rollers across the cricket crease and got them into his viewfinder trying to catch them criss-crossing in front of a big old shed with an odd design on its doors suggesting another bisecting path. It looked potentially interesting but needed a bit more going on to make it swing a bit. A palsied Labrador lolloped into the frame to lift a leg against the shed but the rollers were out of harmony and one of them stopped to shoo the dog away. He had come to see that this was a common problem with the old visual poetry; it had a mind of its own whichever way you looked at it. If the dog had waited till the men passed with their legs well defined and then cocked his own it would have worked. Painters like Graham could invent, but he had to wait for things to happen and this was harder. His tutor had told him that this was a narrow view. He pushed on to the football end where the virile cries of men at their work could be heard: 'That was shite Stan!' ... 'Ah'll fuckin' do you in a minute'... 'Can we have a cuppa tea now boss?' As he got closer he was able to see the man he now knew as Dougie calling across to a young player. 'You'll have to do better than that if you're serious about the first team Pughy.' The lad looked up and threw himself into a tackle with one of the others. 'That's better son,' called Dougie approvingly. 'They need to know you're around.'

Harold hung back and looked for a promising position. He walked halfway up the paddocks to a point where shadows from the grandstand emphasised the action in the rest of the frame. He took a light reading and waited for something to happen. He found that he enjoyed the way the giant shadow threw weight onto the players darting about in the light. He thoroughly enjoyed the next five minutes as he caught some of the movement in a rough harlequin pattern. Then Dougie got them stretching and doing some exercises on the spot. This also fitted in well with his composition and he made fifteen more exposures, then decided to get in closer.

'Can I help you son?' said Dougie as Alan made himself known by standing behind him and clicking his shutter.

'Oh, I've come to take some pictures, I've had a word with Mr Burleson about it.' This bothered Dougie but he tried not to let it show. 'Mr Burleson wants you to take my picture?'

'No no, not just you, not as such...'

'What are you on about? Hang on, didn't I see you last night with Ernie Todd? You're from the Sunday papers. I'd like to know what's going on if you don't mind.' Dougie's demeanour and bluff politeness had settled the players'. All eyes were on the visitor.

'I think Mr Todd got that bit confused...'

'Oh aye?'

'Yes he misheard me, what with the crowd and everything.'

Dougie wasn't convinced. 'There were two of you?'

'Yes, somebody threw my friend onto the pitch.'

'Now that I will believe.'

The players sniggered and the tension cased a little. 'We're both at the art college – I want to do an extended study of life at the club.'

Dougie made a passable impression of the man who'd been given the million-pound banknote in his change. 'I've heard it all now,' he said, then chuckled roughly and advised Harold to get onto the pitch with the players. He felt anxious in a different way now, he'd never been this close to a subject before. The players didn't seem to mind and ignored him as he moved amongst them, winding down under Dougie's sharp eye. They deferred to him, the older man commanded authority. Harold began to mull over some ideas about how he might make him a dominant theme within the photo-essay.

Over at the boiler works Tom Burleson toyed at his desk with sales figures and estimates, but his attention was somewhere else. With the unprecedented interest his wife had been taking in the first team's forward line, in one forward in particular: a southern boy who was too clever by half and might come to rue the day he came to ply his trade among simpler folk. People who put their faith in sturdy fittings and the quiet appliance of settled ways. Bob Mullins had told him that 'Hutchy' was always first out of the bath and keen to get off. She'd been gone for over an hour last night before showing her flushed face for more of 'that nice sherry'. There was also that nuanced lustre about her eyes, which only he could see. He hadn't said anything at the time. How could he, there wasn't anything to say? He'd noticed her clapping at Hutchinson's trickery during the game, when he'd scored she'd smiled and said 'there's no holding him'. He felt wretched, last night's win taken with other results from the teams around them in the table had pushed Northtown back into the promotion race, but all he could think about was his star man's performance off the pitch. He lit up a fresh Kensitas and looked at a piece of paper covered in block capitals. It was from his old pal Robert Thompson, an amiable opportunist who'd put work his way over the years. Did he have any decent ex-works stock for one of his properties, something basic and reliable for a couple of layabouts from the college? He noted the address and this set his active mind down a different track. He decided to take a personal interest in this job, he'd enjoy getting his hands mucky for a change. He didn't phone home to say he'd be late.

Harold had made the most of his luck and pursued the players into the changing room where he was allowed to take some informal shots. One of the men entertained the others by demonstrating how to manipulate his genitalia to resemble a sex-starved turtle. Harold saved his film, this was closer than he wanted to get and would it get him into trouble at the college? Dougie sat grinning like an indulgent old man of the Ming dynasty. With his round bald head and narrowed eyes he was also not far off a giant turtle. Harold thought again about the man with elastic balls and wondered if he could get Dougie's head into the same frame? This pre-occupied him as he cycled home, stirred by his afternoon with the players. As he tied up his bike in the backyard he saw that the kitchen light was on and caught site of Shirley's long blonde hair tied back as she bent over the sink.

'I managed to get some hot water from the woman next door,' she said.

'Oh right, is Graham in? How was your trip??

'No and the trip was fine, thanks.'

'Right – your mother better?'

'My mother's fine. It was my brother's wedding.'

'Yes of course... But didn't you say your mother was bad?'

He decided to bring up the boiler situation directly. 'I've had Mr Thompson round and he assures me he'll have that fixed very soon.'

'What happened, you must have been a bit stuck?'

'I think it just wore out,' he said and walked off to the front room to listen to the news. Something about Czechoslovakia caught his interest, he might talk to Shirley about this as she knew more about politics. He'd heard her talk about Prague at the college. He brought up the topic when she came through herself and learned that it was all very exciting; the government was bringing in freer measures while resisting pressure from the Russians. This was hard for him as apart from a notional understanding that communism was a good thing he was happily unpolitical and these events complicated it. Shirley was confident that Moscow would let them get on with it once they'd got used to the new ideas. They listened to *The Archers* together, then he got up to answer the door. He was surprised to find a smart saloon parked outside and a figure manhandling something through the back of the car.

'Be with you in a minute,' said the man. Harold recognised the voice and when the man stood up he saw that he was the smart bloke from the club he'd dealt with over the project. He'd given him the go-ahead without too much thought and Harold had wondered at the time if it was all going to be so straightforward. Was he going to be asked to fence dodgy goods now, stolen players perhaps? Was this how they were acquired? Promising lads pinched from beneath the noses of bigger clubs to be brainwashed and trained by Mr Peacock after being smuggled across the Pennines in boxes?

'Brought you a new boiler son,' said Burleson. 'Give us a hand.'

'Oh right,' said Harold and told Shirley who held open the doors as the men worked the box through to the kitchen. Then Mr Burleson returned to his car to fetch a canvas bag that clanked and chinked when he put it on the Formica-topped table. He took off his tweed jacket and rolled up his shirt sleeves, then gave them a manly wink and told them he'd soon have the thing 'up and doing'. Harold lent a hand turning off the gas and stood by for further orders as Mr Burleson 'got cracking'. Shirley had gone upstairs but Harold thought he ought to stay.

Mr Burleson regarded the unpacked boiler. 'Time was I could get one of these slapped up and working inside forty minutes. We'll have to get all that muck cleaned off the wall first, probably need a fresh length of pipe in there too. I've got some in the boot.'

Left alone Harold had a look in the tool bag for clues to the ways of the working man. He couldn't help wondering why he was getting the boss though, instead of one of his fitters. 'It's very good of you to come round like this,' he said when Mr Burleson came back with some more piping.

'Oh, I like to keep my hand in. This particular model is a classic you know – the Vital Spark – adapted from one of our earliest makes – the Vesuvius. Problem with that one was it tended to leave a bit of dirt about but once we sorted that out it's been the template for all the rest.' He broke off to look again at the little blue and grey boiler. 'No two are ever really the same and fitting them takes a skilled hand, now you get on yon side and we'll lift her loose to see how she'll hang.'

Harold wondered what he'd got himself into but he knew this was the land of George Stevenson so it must be part of a rich folk tradition he was privileged to share. They put the boiler down again and his gaffer set to work with blue chalk and steel ruler. Harold's role was to hand him things like a theatre nurse awed by the handiwork of a top surgeon. After a short while it became clear that the main task – the fitting of the casing and the connecting of the pipe – had been accomplished. Mr Burleson called a break by sitting back on one of the landlord's ex-tea room chairs and pulling out a packet of cigarettes. He lit up then turned to Harold who was still standing by at the sink. 'When Bobby Thompson got in touch I thought the address rang a bell, something to do with the club so I thought I'd take an interest. I'm very taken by your little project, footballers are like boilers only less predictable. Endlessly fascinating in their ways even though the jobs you want them to do are basically quite simple – as I say I like your idea and feel you should have a free hand but I want you to do me a little favour if you can, I'm sure it would fit in with your aims anyway.'

'Yes, well, yes, I mean I'd like to do something for the club as well.'

'Good, well I want you to do a bit of a feature on our new centre forward Barry Hutchinson. He's a sociable sort of fellow and a super player, but I feel it would be interesting to cover him off the field as well, away from the club even. If you could win his confidence you might want to do a day in the life type of thing – some of the others as well, of course. Anyway, mustn't tell you your business.'

'Oh that's okay, I'm always open to new ideas and it sounds potentially very interesting.'

'Excellent, well we're away to Southend a week on Saturday. You could come with us, it'll be an early start but you could be part of the whole day. I'll square it with the manager, bring a pal if you want.'

'Great.'

'Right let's get this little beauty up and working.'

The telephone rang at Dougie's house. 'He was down the club this morning – did you see him, did he say anything?'

He paused. 'Yes I saw him, said good morning Peacock then went off to find Mullins. I didn't see him at all after that, why, is something the matter?'

'Oh I don't know, he's been in and out all day like a fiddler's elbow. He went in to the works this afternoon and I haven't seen him since.'

Dougie looked at his old watch. 'It's only eight, he's maybe stopped off for a drink, some bit of business.'

Anita paused. 'Yes it's probably that, I'm sure you're right – God he can be a difficult man to live with, not as green as he's cabbage-looking by any means and devious when it comes to business. I'm sure he doesn't suspect anything though, don't you think?'

'Of course he doesn't, why should he?'

'I don't know – a town like this. Maybe we should let things go for a bit, just till we're sure it's safe, what do you say?'

'Well if you–"

'Oh heck here's his car now – I'll ring tomorrow when I can.'

Dougie put down the phone and looked up at the first Mrs Peacock. He wondered if he could ever live with a woman again. Burleson might be a difficult man to live with but at least he was a bloke, a simple enough equation, unlikely to do anything too unexpected. Looking at Linda made him try to be honest with himself, to admit that his arrangement with another man's wife suited him well enough. It wasn't as if she was any kind of replacement and she had a home to go to afterwards. She wasn't another new signing at the club. He'd tried this line on his son when he'd told him all about it but he was very much Linda's lad and had led his father to understand that his view was 'self-serving cobblers'. Then harsher words had meant hurt feelings and the current estrangement. The lad's 'Auntie Reen' was the only person he would see whenever he came back to the town and Dougie was grateful for her careful dealings with him. He knew that she knew what it had all been about and that she'd keep it to herself. Anita didn't know any of this, Reenie knew this too.

It also suited him to be 'Lady Burleson's lover' in another way; knowing he was one up on the boss, the man of substance in the small town with the trades council in his pocket and his fresh air fund for local kiddies. Men like that should look out for themselves and if they couldn't, that was their lookout as well. It had been eight years now – what was he supposed to do, tie a knot in it? He avoided Linda's vulnerable face to see what was in the rest of the photograph. It was taken against the fence in their little back garden, down to her waist in a shapeless cardie wrapping a lighter coloured blouse. Only he knew what she was like beneath them, how poor Anita could never really threaten what had been. At the time it was taken – by who? – they were both in good shape and regulars in a cycling club, then a coal wagon had knocked her down on Addison Street on their way to Newton Aycliffe one sunny morning in March. Three weeks in a coma, then she went. The day after Athletic had been relegated at Rotherham. The way he looked at it he didn't owe anybody anything anymore and if the lad wanted to play at being Softie Walter then he could suit himself, too. It wasn't as if he was any better than he should be, living over the brush with another teacher in Bolton with his hair down over his ears. He thought that was the best place for them and moved away from the hall to switch on his wireless. The set had gone off station again but he twiddled expertly and soon found *Armchair Theatre*. It was about ten minutes in but he got the drift well enough; the usual story about doing the right thing, set this time in war-torn France. Some posh fellow had to choose between going with the woman he loved but betraying his comrades to the enemy, or leave her to undertake his mission of mercy. Dougie couldn't see why he shouldn't do both but in the end the soldier did his duty and Hortense loved him all the more for it. Then the phone went again. 'Dougie it's me,' said a breathy Anita.

'Right,' said Dougie.

'He's gone again.'

'Gone?'

'Out. Again... say something Dougie. Are you still on the line?'

'Yes, yes... well he can go out if he wants, can't he? Did he say where he was going?'

'To check something – that's where he said he'd been before, fitting a boiler and he'd forgotten to do something.'

'Well that sounds right enough, doesn't it? What's the worry?'

'It was the way he said it.'

Dougie held the receiver away from him so she couldn't hear what he'd muttered. 'How'd you mean, pet?'

'All salty, sharp. You'd need to know him but it wasn't lost on me.'

'Salty?'

'Yes – sharp and peppy.'

'Just tell me what he said.'

'Well, he came in with his tool bag and his tie loose. I asked him if he'd been working late and he looked at me with a smile and says "I'm in the process of sorting out an old boiler". Then he said that he liked to keep his hand in to make sure he hadn't lost it. Then he smiled at me again and went on about older models being best and having a surprisingly warm flame, how all you had to do to keep it constant was give the right attention.'

'Well. What then?'

'He sat down in front of the telly as normal. Then after a bit takes it into his head to go out again, like I said. He knows something, I've said before how devious he can be, haven't I Doug?'

'Yes, you have pet, but that stuff he said – it could just be gas man's talk. I've heard him talking shop down at the club, gets quite keen on it sometimes...'

'Yes but it was the way he was saying it, saying it to me. Saying it like he was daring me to come back with something.

They were not honeyed words Douglas, and there are some hefty spanners in that bag.'

The following Wednesday Eunice and Reenie were washing the balls as they reviewed the weekly news. 'He goes back without seeing him then?' asked Eunice.

'Aye, still not talking. I think they're both crackers but I don't say owt.'

'So he's still carrying on with Lady Bottomley?'

'Aye,' sighed Reenie. 'Pair of daft beggars – now what about our lot last Saturday, back to Earth with a bump or what?'

'Aye,' agreed Eunice. 'Got carried away with themselves after beating Pools, it's a poor show if you follow that by losing at home to Halifax. You could see it coming though after ten minutes; Sproates looked a yard off the pace and Stanton's not a ball winner in midfield, their sweeper brushed him aside time and again. Hutchy got no service from the wings and once they'd scored Thompson put up the white flag.'

Reenie nodded and reached for the Vim. 'Ah reckon Big Bill's had it, time to put him out to grass in the Northern League – Bedlington Terriers would suit him.'

Eunice laughed. 'Big Bill's terrier days are long gone, mind he's going to do someone a serious injury before long. They say that Pools lad's lucky he can still play.'

They shared a pursed-up nod. Thompson's career was as good as over. 'So,' said Reenie. 'Southend away on Saturday. If we can win there we're back in with a chance. Do you fancy going down, they've chartered a couple of buses?'

'Could do. Have they altered the design on the Vim again?'

CHAPTER FOUR

NEWS FROM THE NORTH

On Harold's new television Mike Neville was wrapping up a feature on the walkout at Head Wrightson's steelworks. The genial journalist looked shaken at the prospect of revolution taking root at Redcar. 'What do you think Shirl?' asked Graham. 'Will the Prague Spring spread to Spennymoor?'

'Hard to say, but keep your sketchbook handy, all revolutions need a witness. Never underestimate the state's capacity for revision – whole lives erased by the stroke of a pen.'

Harold couldn't help himself. 'Wouldn't it be the stroke of a rubber and wasn't Uncle Joe keen on a spot of the old revision? Maybe Graham could get work retouching the pictures when your lot get in.'

'Harry you're hopeless, everything is a political act – just think about photography, power, representation, the whole business of appropriating a slice of someone else's life.'

She's got a new boyfriend, thought Harold, not one of our lot by the sound of it. He'd spotted her with an older-looking bloke in Binns recently and wondered who he was. 'I've never really thought that's what I've been doing. I just like the way things look sometimes.'

Graham nodded at this. 'I suppose that might be why you would want to paint a picture.'

She sighed quickly and stood up to switch off the weather forecast. 'Well why do you choose to take or paint a certain thing and when it's done who gets to see it?'

After a pause Graham went first. 'You're drawn to something by a feeling, something you want to celebrate in some way, I think. It's hard to say really – as far as I can see anyone can look at it afterwards, if they want to.'

That seemed to be it from Graham and they turned to Harold. 'I've been thinking that what I do and why I do it is very political, not just in a journalistic family of man sort of way but at a deeper level. I think it's possible to rearrange the spaces in a frame to tell a truth about ourselves. Maybe it's possible to make the world a better place by catching it like that, drawing attention to things we'd normally miss and recording them. Isn't that a political act?'

Graham was looking at him carefully, he'd never heard the like of that from his chum before. Shirley was also looking at him. 'I never knew you were such a romantic,' she said. 'Perhaps you believe we can sit in our back gardens after a day's work counting our potatoes and writing poems while our children run free.'

Harold wondered what had happened to the girl with a quilted anorak who painted watercolours. She stuck up prints by Cannedwhatsit now and said the kind of things she'd just said. 'Well,' he said. 'What... what do you mean? We haven't got a back garden, and as for...'

'Charles Ives said that, you two would have got on with him.'

'Never heard of him,' said Graham mildly.

'Someone was telling me about him, he was an American composer who sold insurance during the day. He was a real romantic, wanted the back garden to be a better place.'

'Not a Russian then,' said Harold.

'No Harold not a Russian. Freedom of expression can be a bit of a luxury.'

'Some wonderful painters though,' put in Graham. 'Chagal, Kokoshka... and so forth.'

'So who was telling you about Charles Doodah?' asked Harold.

'Oh, someone I met through Bob Collins at SocSoc – I fancy a cup of tea, anyone else want one now that our kitchens back in business?' She got up as she said this and was through to the kettle before they could answer. Graham looked quizzical and Harold rolled his eyes, then told him about the Southend trip, did he fancy coming along? He said that once had been enough and Harold remembered he'd been dealt roughly by the crowd. It was one subject you really needed a feeling for and Graham didn't. Shirley eventually came back with a full tea tray. Harold was touched to see that she still liked to do that.

'Shirley,' said Graham. 'The Russians are good footballers aren't they? Remember the World Cup, Lev Yashin.'

'Are they? All I remember about the World Cup is the Scottish bloke getting drunk next door and going on about the bent linesman – who was Russian now you mention it. I don't think he wanted England to win, how did we get on to ball games anyway?'

'Harold's going to Southend on Saturday with the Northtown team bus, there's a spare seat, fancy going?'

Shirley put her cup down. 'I'm free on Saturday, it might be interesting now you mention it.' She sipped some more while

Harold glared at Graham. 'Yes, why not – they'll bring us back presumably.'

'You were a long time on the phone, Tom,' said Anita.

He flopped down on the sofa. 'It's that bloody fool from Chapmans wanting reassurance that our lot won't be coming out in sympathy with the daft beggars up the road. I told him it's a long way from Leningrad to Thornaby but his father can remember the twenties. Bad times for boilermen.'

'Weren't our lot up in the second division then?'

'We were indeed – heady days for a season or two. You'd need to ask Dougie Peacock about that, I dare say he was a lad on the terraces – he's an odd fellow you know, the other day I could have sworn...'

'Look Tom, Mike Neville's come on about this strike business.' The news claimed their attention for fifteen minutes, then Anita went to put the finishing touches to the tea. 'Ready dear!' she called after a while, turning off *The Archers* as Dan had gone down with indigestion and she didn't want Tom put off her guilt-rinsed casserole. Halfway through the meal he turned the talk towards the Southend fixture.

'I dare say Hutchinson will want to show his southern friends a trick or two. He's done very well for us so far, mind, full marks to Mullins for getting him. Do you remember the way he turned the Hartlepool defence, had them chasing shadows?'

'Was that the second goal? Wasn't there a bit of a to-do after the young lad scored?'

'That was the winner, Hutchinson took the penalty though – marvelous save from their keeper, you wouldn't think a big fellow like that could throw himself about.'

Anita freed some meat from her teeth with a deft application of top lip and tongue. Tom shoved another wedge of sausage into his own maw and gazed ruminatively at the works calendar on the wall, it featured images of boilers from history. March's picture was an artist's impression of the little known 'Vulcan's Forge' 1885 model. A solid-looking construction, though he was glad he wouldn't have to take his chances with it these days. There were some lovely touches to it; delicate ironwork and plenty of shiny plate. Something useful and beautiful, a work of art.

She liked to talk football with him, anything to get him off pipes and water tables. 'The main thing I remember about that game was that unfortunate incident when their man had to go off.'

'These things happen, football can be a tough old game.'

'Is he all right now, do you know?'

'Mullins tells me there's no harm done.'

'Is it right that we could go up if we win on Saturday?'

'Not directly, but a win would put us in a good position because they're above us and if Lincoln lose at Halifax, who beat us last week – well, it's all to play for.'

'And we're going along with the troops, on the bus?'

'Yes, I thought it would be a good idea to show solidarity, once more into the breach and all that. The players like to feel the board's goodwill.' Anita began to side away and pull on her rubber gloves. 'Oh don't do that – I'll clear up, then I need to pop out to have another word with Ted Chapman. You go through, there's a good play on the BBC tonight.'

Anita was unable to settle to the play – some far-fetched tale about cowboys in Castleford – and got straight on the phone as soon as Tom's car took off down the road. 'He's gone out again,' she said.

Dougie sighed audibly this time. 'Well what of it, a man can go out can't he – did he say where he was going?'

'Off to see Ted Chapman over some trouble at work. I think there might be a strike on, there was something in the news, do you know anything?'

'I might have heard something – who's Ted Chapman?'

'One of his work cronies, I believe he runs a factory at Northallerton. There's definitely trouble in the air because Mike Neville was talking about it.'

'Oh well, that settles it – listen Nita, it all sounds right enough. It sounds like normal behaviour in the circumstances. Captains of industry standing, if it comes to a walkout his pal from Hartlepool'll be first in line to start shooting strikers.'

She tittered softly at this and relaxed a bit. 'Hey, you know this match on Saturday down in London?'

'Southend.'

'Yes anyway, we'll all be on the bus together won't we?'

'Will we? First I've heard of it.'

'It's all set apparently. Leading from the front, he says, tally-ho boys and off for the day. I think he's not been right since the night he went off to fix that boiler, oh and there's a photographer coming with us plus guest. Will this be the one you mentioned?'

Dougie hesitated. 'Well,' he said eventually. 'We'd best sit apart on the bus.'

'Well of course you clown, I'll naturally be sitting with him. What do you think he's up to and what's all this with travelling photographers?'

'Oh, he's just some lad from the college, forget about him – if he steps out of line one of the players'll chin 'im. Listen pet, what I think is Tom's all fired up because the team's up for promotion, so next season he might be rubbing shoulders with a whole new set of business types. Also, being chairman of a winning team does you well as it is, everybody wants to be in on it – explains why he's cooking up something now with Ted Chapman. That's how these things work, why people put money into football clubs, put good money into Northtown Athletic. It can generate a surprising return and your Tom's a businessman, and a good one, don't forget that. We'll just have to sit tight a bit, that's all.'

'Oh Dougie, just talking to you makes it all seem simpler, whatever happens we must always be here for each other.'

'Of course pet – now, next Saturday everything as normal eh?'

'Yes – see you then.'

Dougie put down the phone and ducked quickly away from the picture on the wall. As he sat by the wireless, shrewd midfielders troubled the back line of his mind.

At his family home Brian Atkinson lay on the edge of sleep with conflicting reflections. He'd been horrified by some of what he'd seen during the last few league games with the first team. He thought they were just joking when they talked of 'sorting out Twinkletoes' before the Hartlepool match, but Bill Thompson had gone directly for the player's ankle. The really shocking thing had been how skilfully he'd done it – the only real skill he'd shown all game. Some of their lads had seen it but not the gormless ref, so it all blew up again after his goal and he found himself ready to fight. This had shaken him a bit and he'd cried after he got home. He knew Hancocks from their youth league days, he was a top lad, and bound for the big time, if he survived at this level. Then there'd been that bald guy from Halifax who threatened to break his leg if he nutmegged him again. He'd wondered if he meant it but it had been dinned into him time and again that you were finished if they knew they could intimidate you. He did him again near the end, to put in a cross which Guthrie headed over and the Halifax guy shook his hand at the end and told him not to be put off because the crowd loves a flying winger. He asked Sproates about him afterwards and learned that he was an old Wales international called Watkins playing out his days with Halifax. When he told his captain what Watkins had said he'd laughed and reflected that the 'old twat' had sent a few wingers flying in his time and stupid Guthrie should have buried that cross. He knew he was doing well and was brave enough but he'd had no idea how rough professional football could be. He'd thought he would enjoy it much more than he was doing – and the next match was a big one, away to the best side in the division. Mr Mullins had told him he would probably put him on during the second half.

kie Deacon, Feethams, March 1983. Dickie Deacon has been connected with Darlington for over 30 years as a player, coach
d physiotherapist. A vital force in the clubs development.

CHAPTER FIVE

SEX AND DRUGS AND SAUSAGE ROLLS

Harold walked Shirley down to the ground through Green Park early on Saturday morning, taking some pictures on the way; a few panoramic shots of the town from the hill then some of the budding trees with her in between them. She looked suitably dreamy, like a princess awakened from fretful slumber to look on the world anew. 'Do we have to do this, I've just stood in some dog shit?' said the Princess.

'No, all right let's get cracking, bus sets off at seven.'

'Are you going to talk like that all day then?'

'Like what?'

'One of the Likely Lads – the daft one.'

'Eh? Oh look, wipe your boot on that long grass.'

He hoped that Shirley wouldn't be awkward with the people on the bus or start talking about Rosa Luxembourg. She'd got herself up very nicely though in her kinky boots, Levi jeans and old flyer's jacket. As they moved into the town she asked to stop for a copy of *The Guardian* and ten Number Six. 'I didn't't know you smoked,' he said. She told him she was getting into bad habits and smiled. 'Well you'll be in good company, most of the players smoke, and drink from what I've heard.'

'They do sound an interesting lot,' said Shirley.

The area around the cricket pitch had several buses parked on it. From a distance figures hovered around them like slow bees at a hive. As they drew closer Harold saw that they were already crammed with supporters and the engines were running. 'Which is our bus?' she asked.

'The team coach'll be by the grandstand over there,' he said, crossing his fingers. They passed the small convoy of old coaches and the football end where he saw a smaller, more modern vehicle. Dougie was talking to one of the older women he remembered from his first day. He was stressing a point by moving an open palm outward near his chest. He seemed quite upset about something. The woman noticed Harold and he heard her ask Dougie who 'these two' were.

Dougie looked over to them without smiling. 'Our photographer plus friend, by special invitation apparently.' Then he addressed Harold directly. 'You'd best get on – sit at the back and save a place for me.'

They got on and did as they'd been told. 'He didn't't seem very friendly,' said Shirley.

'Ah well, it's match day and an important one. Everybody needs to be focused.'

'What on, being obnoxious?'

'No no it's not that Shirl, it's more the silence of men and shouldn't be misunderstood. Soccer is a non-verbal creativity, there'll also be anxiety in the air. It's a serious business.'

'Well as long as it's silent,' she said sniffily and pulled out her paper. Harold placed his camera bag to reserve Dougie's seat and looked through the window. From their spot in the car park he could see the town's river through a big gap in the fence. There was an upturned pram being lapped gently and he pondered whether the waters were tidal then decided they couldn't be. He could also see across to the Edwardian terrace on the other bank. He thought he'd like to live in a house like that one day. The bus tilted slightly as one of the players boarded and from Shirley's side he could see them all filing out from the back of the stand. He recognised some of them and remembered what Mr Burleson had said about Hutchinson, who came out last laughing with one of the others. Harold caught the end of the banter as they got on – 'things just snowballed from there' – said Hutch and his mate laughed again. The coach was nearly full and there was a pleasant hubbub of conversation and shifting about in seats. Shirley seemed to brighten up a bit. 'They all seem chatty enough,' she said. Then Dougie climbed up with the woman he'd been talking to followed by Mr Mullins and a few others. The chatter subsided when Mr Burleson came on last preceded by an elegant woman in a fur coat. He helped her off with it then showed her to her seat and sat down beside her. Dougie sat with Harold and his friend, said 'Hello pet' and sat with Shirley. As soon as everyone was settled Mr Mullins stood up to scan the party. Satisfied with what he'd seen he clapped his hands and said, 'Full steam ahead.' And they were off.

By the time they'd reached the A1 the conversational level had risen and everyone seemed to be enjoying themselves. Shirley was chatting quite happily with Eunice and Dougie had his nose in *The Guardian*. The phrase 'poetry of departures' kept washing up in Harold's mind from somewhere, but the fearfulness he'd felt as they were all getting on the bus was beginning to disperse with the lulling movement. He'd always liked looking through windows from somewhere safe inside and, as he thought about this, it seemed to involve his mother chatting to her mother off to his left in a bus in a blurry tableaux that seemed to be both in and outside of him. It would be raining in this image and they would be passing the town library in their bus and he'd be happy, but something else too. Content? Safe in his skin? He wasn't sure but he liked the idea and was pretty sure it had really happened once upon a time. Outside he could see a big aerodrome near Catterick, men prancing about near a plane, then fields again and someone on a grey tractor. He tried to make a pattern of it and blinked when he felt he had. Dougie put down his paper. 'You like taking pictures then son?' he said.

'Yeah – I'm hoping to get some good ones today.'

'Aye well, listen son. You stick close by me when we get there, Eunice can look after your young lady and when I tell you to put your camera away and keep your head down. Especially before the match and at half-time, other times use your common sense. I'm sure they teach you some of that at college.'

'Yes, I'll try not to get in the way. What do you think of the team's chances today, is Hutchinson playing?'

'Hard to say, a point would be a good result down there but the trouble is we have to win to stand any real chance of promotion after last week's result. If Hutchy does get his game he'll have to do better than last match.'

This was the most the older man had ever said to him. Harold pushed his luck. 'He's a good player though, isn't he?'

'He can play right enough when he wants to, anyway you just mind what I said. Footballers can be a funny lot.' Dougie turned away to say something to Eunice and Shirley looked over and smiled.

They were now passing through Nottinghamshire, the home of Nottingham Forest who everybody hated for some reason. As far as he knew people didn't sing about Southend United but he liked their nickname 'The Shrimpers' and, as Northtown's was 'The Shunters', he looked forward to the match report. If

Northtown lost – 'got beat' – they might be caught in a net or sunk without trace. If they won Southend might be sidelined as they missed the points. Drawn games were invariably 'honours even'. He drifted off as his neighbour's voice took on a warm burred tone during an anecdote concerning next door's cat. The next thing he knew was Shirley rubbing his arm. They were the only ones on the bus.

'What's happened, where's Dougie gone?'

'Bishops Stortford.'

'Why? I'm supposed to be under his thumb.'

'I think you mean his wing, and we're all here. Stopped for a break as we're ahead of schedule, fancy a Kunzel cake and a sausage roll?'

'Yes, I'm with you now.'

Harold's treats were to be found inside a cavernous roadside cafe called Laurie's, used by drivers taking the eastern run out of Harlow and occasional coach parties venturing into the deep South. He ordered the food and two teas while Shirley found them a seat with the fur coat lady and Barry Hutchinson. 'Barry's been telling us all about southern ways,' she said when Harold joined them. 'Apparently they keep coal in the bath too.'

Shirley was laughing and Barry winked at him as he sat down. 'You're going to record this historic match then?'

Before he could think of something to say to this mythical man of football the lady spoke. 'Oh, you're the young man Tom was telling me about. I'm Mrs Burleson, please call me Anita.' Sundry pleasantries accompanied the best pastry Harold had tasted south of Wetherby; then Barry, who'd been amusing them, suggested he take their pictures as they were. He soon had his stuff out and took a light reading to set his exposure. He took a formal one with both women smiling demurely as Barry spread his arms expansively round their shoulders. When they thought he'd finished he took some less posed ones of the players as they talked, even managing to catch Dougie laughing at something Mr Mullins said to him. Before common sense told him to pack away his camera he snapped one more of Barry with Mrs Burleson; she was leaning towards him sharing a confidence with Shirley beside him the composition nicely facing the other way as she sucked on a number six. He put his precious Yashica FX camera down and picked up his tea. It was tepid and he tried to ignore the chipped saucer as he swallowed it in one go. He looked around and saw that most of the party were on their feet and making for the door, though Anita was still in thrall to whatever it was that Barry was telling her. He took some ribbing from the rest when they got back on the bus and Dougie grunted 'flash pillock' in a voice that seemed to carry.

The rest of the journey across Essex felt like an extended traffic jam and when they got there Southend looked a drab spot. Harold couldn't see the sea but there were some fed-up seagulls surfing dully in the wind like grey stuff over a bonfire. He experienced a hair-trigger belch of seagull sausage meat, as the aftertaste marinated for him with the upholstery and fag smoke, he tried not to chuck all over the back seat. They seemed to be stuck for ages in a side street before reaching a more open area with a sign welcoming them to Roots Hall. Mr Mullins stood to address the men. 'Straight through to the dressing rooms and look out for a little fella with a brown envelope. That'll be Feathers with your complementaries – be back on the bus for six thirty.'

'Come on son,' said Dougie. 'Eunice can take care of the young lady and remember what I said, once the gaffer comes in to get them ready keep your head down.' Harold filed down the coach with his mentor to stand with him as he counted out several large wicker baskets from the storage space beneath the vehicle. Some young lads appeared by the main buildings where quite a few more people were milling around. He sensed a large crowd assembling.

Southend looked to be a more go-ahead place than Northtown and the people seemed sharper, more watchful. When he strayed off to buy a Mars bar the woman had called him 'Jock' and someone had called out 'woolly backs' at the players as they made for the entrance to the dressing room area. Then when he tried to get some pictures of the people against a corrugated iron wall he was advised to 'naff off back to the long grass'. He went to find Dougie who was chatting happily with a small old man who had a crinkly face but no teeth as far as he could see, Harold thought he must be the man with the free tickets. Dougie spotted Harold and ushered him through to the area beneath the stand, which was bigger than Northtown's and had carpets. 'He's a character he is, a proper old Pikey,' said Dougie. 'Place would collapse without him – every club needs its Feathers.'

Harold had the sense not to ask who Northtown's Pikey was and followed Dougie down to the away dressing room. The little fellow who they'd just left was waiting for them there, this made Harold wonder if Roots Hall was got up like the Old Professor's castle in Rupert Bear where sprites and goblins were able to move about the place at speed via secret doors and hidden air shafts. He half expected Rosa Lea the pig to put in an appearance waving a football rattle. Anything seemed possible in this dim-lit world of silent understanding between people of the underworld. Dougie and Feathers shared a knowing nod with pursed lips as he passed Dougie an envelope and opened a door. This was truly the hard won wisdom of men and Harold felt awed by them. He hadn't a clue what was going on, but knew it must mean something.

The dressing room was a familiar sight. Several men sat trance-like in their underpants as others threw toilet rolls about, Barry Hutchinson stood fully dressed reading a copy of the *Southend Sentinel*. Harold took a nice one of that complete with flying bog roll, he hoped, and some fascinating activity involving Dougie handing out various creams and ointments, tying shin pads and practicing what looked to be an ancient form of physiotherapy on a player who seemed to be really enjoying the process. Dougie was very much in command of the ship as he offered mannish advice and lent seasoned experience. All the players listened and Harold was filled with respect for their coach, he was also delighted with what he reckoned to have caught on film. He took one more picture of Dougie explaining something important to the man he recognised as Big Bill, then Mr Mullins entered so he made himself scarce by sitting in the small toilet at the other end of the room. He'd only just sat down when Mr Mullins told him to shift as he needed to 'pump ship' and told him to sit next to Barry Hutchinson on the end of the bench.

What happened next clarified quite a bit of what Dougie had said and done since they'd sat together on the bus. There was a clear change in the atmosphere and the players' attitude, even Hutchinson looked at his knees then Mullins began his team talk. His general impressions of the manager up to this point had been of a genial though detached figure, content for Dougie to oversee day-to-day management of the players. Now he could see what was entailed in regulating a band of disparate and unruly men into an effective team capable of remarkable things with a football. Raw fear seemed to have a lot to do with it although Mullins didn't't actually shout at them, not in strict acoustical terms, and it wasn't so much what he said – predictable invective laced with lavatorial encouragement to kick them whenever the ref wasn't looking. It was simply the obvious message that Mr Mullins was not a man to be messed with and because his unmissable hard man menace was so clearly being kept on a leash. It was something about him, he could have been reading them Dante in the original, but by the time he was done they would still have marched into battle fired by his personality.

Harold sat where he'd been put till the last player had clacked out of the dressing room, then Dougie fixed him with a gruff wink and Harold followed him out. The stadium was packed with spectators, faces filled the paddocks like frogspawn and the stand was crowded. He managed to catch sight of Shirley's jacket and saw that she was with Eunice and Mrs Burleson. As the players from both sides trotted about and practiced passing the tannoy system crackled and announced a special request 'for our eccentric visitors'. Alan Price came on to sing about 'Simon Smith and His Amazing Dancing Bear'. The cheeky reference was lost on the crowd, Dougie seemed not to hear it as he sorted through his kit bag for some bandaging. In fact he and Mr Mullins seemed to have forgotten all about Harold as they got ready in their dugout, so he took up a crouching position to the far side where he watched the action for the first twenty minutes or so. Southend seemed to have the ball for a lot of the time and looked certain to score. Most of the Northtown players were stuck in their own half and two of them had already been booked for fouling the same Southend player – a short nippy bloke who he could see was running rings round Big Bill. Then Sproates got the ball but, instead of thumping it upfield, he took it past a Southend man, paused, then passed across the field to Hutchinson who cushioned the ball with his thigh, ran forward and shot from a distance. The ball clapped cleanly off the crossbar and went out of play. The crowd applauded and Harold heard someone say that Hutch was 'too good for this lot'. He noted that this sudden attack by Northfield changed the pattern of play as Southend became more cautious, then Hutchinson got away again to pass to Guthrie – but he blasted the ball wide. He turned his camera on Hutchinson but he didn't see much of the ball again then the whistle went for half-time. Harold was shocked by how quickly it had passed and ran to catch up with Dougie, who was heading for the dressing room before the players trooped off.

Mugs of tea stood on an old table beneath a large mirror, most of the players spooned in more sugar as they panted like cattle. One of the defenders called Roberts had picked up a dead leg and lay on the stone floor for Dougie to see to it. He took a few pictures of this and noticed that if he used the mirror he could work more discretely. He stood at the correct angle for this, then Mullins came in. He got one of him quickly then sat down where he'd been put before. The manager continued to fascinate him; this time his aura was quietly commanding as he talked to each player in turn, showing a proper concern for his men and approval for the way they'd 'kept shape' during a first half he dubbed a 'right humdinger'. Dougie finished his coaxing and rubbing with Roberts, who stood to trot on the spot – 'Ah'll soon run it off, like'.

'Right,' said Mullins. 'It'll be a tougher second half and their big defenders might come forward, but that's when we can do them on the break. They know we've not just come for a point – see the way they slowed back after Hutch rattled the bar – so it could be an open match. It's there for us to win if we're patient and keep it tight at the back. Anyway, well done lads, we couldn't have asked for more, eh Doug?'

Dougie nodded curtly. 'Watch that little lad on the right though, he can be a handful.'

Harold felt happy to be where he was, in the company of men, rallied and nurtured by tough love and dreams of glory. A band of brothers. He wanted them to win and felt a pang of anticipation when a loud buzzer signaled the second half. Sproates warmed the chill room with a rousing entreaty and led them back out to polite applause, which crescendoed when Southend followed them. Harold noticed Dougie and Mullins share a tight smile and decided he too should step up his game. He wanted to record some of the goings-on in the dugout once play restarted, and felt confident that his own skills of unobtrusive observation meant that no one would take much notice of him.

Southend were still getting more possession and testing Northtown's goalie who was 'earning his corn' as Dougie put it. He felt that Southend were certain to breakthrough and edged closer to the pitch to get an angle on the dugouts. He was pleased by what he could see; plenty of expressive hand gestures, mouthed obscenity and much getting up and sitting down. It was all nicely set off by young Atkinson who was perched beside a manic Mullins like a choirboy awaiting his solo. Dougie spent a lot of time shouting and waving his fist. He snapped away for about three minutes then remembered his special assignment. Hutchinson was standing quite nearby chatting with a Southend man near the centre spot. He took a boring one, then the ball shot over their heads and the focus shifted to the Southend goal as Hutchinson put on an amazing burst of pace to catch the ball before it left play on the far side; he then looked to be dawdling, but his marker stood off him enabling several blue shirts to dash forward. Harold heard someone in the crowd say 'Hey watch out!' then Hutchinson pushed the ball through the player's legs to Roberts who hit a fierce shot which Southend's goalie pushed round the post. Corner to the visitors. He heard the same voice lamenting that 'this lot'll score soon, you watch –our defense don't know what to do with him'. Fidler walked across to take the kick but didn't seem to be in much of a hurry, then Harold heard Dougie barking out something to Sproates. The captain sprinted across to Fidler taking a Southend man with him, Fidler shaped to swing the ball into the goal mouth, but cleverly tapped it beyond Sproates to Guthrie, who crossed the ball for Thompson who dived bravely to head the ball in for a goal. His momentum took him into the net as well, via the goalpost. The away supporters went mad, Dougie dashed from the dugout with his bag for emergencies and Harold turned without looking to crash into a sprinting linesman who wanted to explain something to Mr Mullins. The official went down with a howl and strangled cry to Harold that his knee was 'knackered now'. The section of the crowd with the best view found it amusing and it was pointed out that this was a tactic Northtown sometimes used. Harold helped him up and rubbed at his knee as he'd seen Dougie do with injured players. He was waved away impatiently and asked what he was doing on the line anyway. 'I'm covering the match,' said Harold.

'Well,' said the limping linesman. 'Fuck off behind the goal and stay there.'

He could see a cross-looking Mullins approaching so he walked round the cinder track towards the Northtown goal as fast as he could. He encountered Dougie helping an anguished Bill Thompson off the pitch. 'Where are you off to son?' he asked.

'Just over there,' answered Harold.

Fortunately Mullins caught up with Dougie and helped him with their battered centre half who was knackered too. Harold heard the manager say he would 'have to throw the kid on now' as he edged round behind the goal where the press photographer was sitting. Les from *The Sentinel* introduced himself and they became acquainted via Harold's long-standing friendship with Ernie Todd who knew Les, then Harold remembered that Big Bill had actually scored a goal and that 'they' were winning. Atkinson had come on in place of the injured Thompson, but Hutchinson seemed to have gone into a defensive position beyond Harold's reach. He trained his camera on the home crowd who were moaning and waving their arms. He had become familiar with how close to sentimentality football fans could get; they loved the players but disappointment was the common outcome so it never took much for them to seem tired and emotional.

It was all happening at the other end again and Southend's goalie was jumping on the spot just in front of them and pacing around his penalty box. It became clear that something was happening across at the Northtown goal. The ref eree had stopped play and the crowd was baying. 'Looks like a penalty,' said Les. Several men from either team had surrounded the referee and were pointing and shouting. He waved them all away and went to consult the linesman Harold had tangled with earlier and, after much grave chin-wagging, pointed to the goalmouth to a chorus of disapproval from the terraces. Les explained, 'He's not given the penalty, it's a goal kick. Problem was that the linesman's struggling to keep up and can't have seen much –looks like he's limping now.'

'Oh,' said Harold. 'But they're sure to score soon?'

'Be hell to pay if they don't, looked like a clear penalty to me.'

The crowd began to barrack the disabled linesman and Harold hoped the ball would stay down at the other end. It did for the next ten minutes, then Atkinson gained possession and went past a defender from just inside his half, Sproates ran to his left and called for a pass but, just as he was about to roll the ball over to him, Atkinson was barged off the ball and the other linesman raised his flag for a free kick to Northtown. Now the action was within Harold's view but he was too excited to take any pictures. Most of the Northtown players had come forward and he could hear the terse remarks of the defenders'. Stanton lofted the ball into the goalmouth and three players went up to head it. The ball was obscured, then it flashed towards the net where a Southend player managed to hack it off the line. The players moved to follow it but Atkinson had positioned himself just outside the penalty box and managed to head the ball upwards, then bring it quickly under control as it fell to his feet; he went past one man but another clattered him and the linesman waved his flag again. The ball ran free and Guthrie kicked it past the goalkeeper as most of the players waited for the referee to blow for the foul. He signaled a goal instead and once more found himself in conflict with the Southend fans and several of their players. Les explained; 'Played the advantage there, you shouldn't stop until he blows up for a foul.'

It wasn't long after this that the whistle did go to end the game. The crowd was a sporting lot and applauded both sets of players off, though Harold did hear someone saying that the officials should be in a suitable condition to run the line. He hung back pestering Les for advice about film speeds until the coast was clear enough for him to sneak down the tunnel. He decided not to show his face in the dressing room and loitered in the connecting corridor. There were plenty of figures moving here and there and, as no one seemed to notice him, Harold thought he'd have a look around. A man with a metal bucket apologised for bumping him as he passed and this made Harold feel that he belonged. Then he heard someone asking if one of the physios would have a look at the linesman's leg, so he went up some stairs which took him round a corner then up to the top of the grandstand where he had a nice view of the arena. The pitch was clear and the floodlights had come on, so he thought he'd round off his photo essay with a few from there. He used the structures and tiers of seating in the foreground to frame the composition, then decided they'd look better with some human forms in there somewhere. He panned around from behind the wooden tip-up chairs. There was something happening over in the facing stand but too far off to make anything of; he was about to go back downstairs when he heard some seats smacking back below him and ducked out of sight. It was a man and woman who looked around herself quickly. Her brown coat and sharp profile gave her the air of a flustered hen. Harold focused on the scene as the man stood up to embrace her, clicked his shutter then withdrew into the shadows.

Down below Eunice and Reenie were chatting to Feathers who was explaining how the referee had cost his side the game and making his points by kicking a metal bucket. Harold walked across to the little group where he was immediately joined by Dougie, who said he wanted a word with him. 'Never mind that,' said Reenie. 'Have you seen her ladyship?'

'Eh? Oh, I think I did spot her somewhere... now listen son if you're serious about...'

'Dougie,' said Eunice. 'This is important. I've told his nibs we'll keep an eye out.'

'Well what makes you think I've any idea?'

She looked at him but said nothing, and Dougie left them with another comment to Harold about the need for a word. 'Don't worry about him son,' she said. 'I've known Dougie

Peacock since he was a lad selling his dad's pies on Stockton market – they soon went soft.'

Shirley appeared and laughed at Eunice's comments. 'Harry I've really enjoyed this, wasn't it exciting?'

Eunice chuckled wryly at this. 'Yon linesman was just wild about Harry – a crucial moment that was.'

'Oh flip, you saw that.'

'The whole crowd saw it, mind Dougie's no one to point the finger –we know all about that.'

'Are you all right?' Shirley asked him.

'Yes thanks, I suppose we should head for the bus.'

'Mmm… seems a shame to go home so soon,' she said and pushed a cigarette into her mouth. Then she wandered over in the general direction of the dressing rooms. Harold found a spare table and began to unpack his bag, winding off his exposed film and generally putting things in order. He found an unused roll of Ilford TRI-X Pan he'd forgotten about and rolled it on carefully in case there was more material to come, then he found his uneaten Mars bar and sat for a while listening to someone's transistor broadcasting another reading of the day's results. A man with a posh voice told the nation that 'Northfield's splendid win has elevated them to third in the table'. He looked forward to a cup of tea then the comfort of a warm bus home.

The volume of people was seeping away and he saw some of the players drifting off to the coach. He recognised Sproates with his arm round Atkinson's shoulder and Dick Burton the goalie with a red mark down one side of his face. Then Shirley appeared with Barry Hutchinson in tow. 'Listen Harry, let's make a night of it, Barry's got some mates down here.'

'What about getting back?' he said, feeling a twit.

'Don't worry about that Harry,' said Barry. 'It's up to us how we get home just so long as we're on time for the next training session. We don't have to travel on the bus – Mullins won't be there, he's gone to the hospital with Bill.'

'Yeah,' said Harold. 'Why not?' He could evade Dougie for another few days but what kind of entertainment did Barry Hutchinson have up his crafty sleeve? And what was Shirley playing at? Barry winked as he sauntered off to tell Captain Sproates what was happening.

'There's a pub round the corner, he'll meet us there in half an hour,' said Shirley briskly.

'I was just thinking I could do with a drink,' said Harold gamely.

The Moon Under Water didn't match Harold's expectations; no wooden partitions and polished glass, no doughty barmaid from a Bill Brandt study pulling through a local brew. At first sight everyone seemed to be perched on poufs around low plastic tables. Long John Baldry was belting out *Let the Heartaches Begin* from the flashest jukebox he'd ever seen. At the bar an unsmiling landlord asked him curtly what he wanted, then stared at him. Shirley was sitting in a corner near the door. He ordered a Babycham to go with his half of Double Diamond. He joined her and immediately began to fret at the likely cost of a night out in the South. She told him not to worry. Then Barry appeared with his friend Thommo who walked with a limp and had a full beard. His hair was quite long too and when he sat down next to Harold, he smelled a bit off. When Barry joined them with more drinks he learned that Thommo was an ex-player who'd had to retire early following a nasty injury and now managed beat groups. He had a van parked outside and when they'd finished their drinks would drive them all off to Canvey Island where one of his stable was playing. They would get in free as his guests. Shirley showed warm enthusiasm for this and Harold wondered what had happened to the girl who liked Stravinsky and somebody called Mandlestam. Barry was funny about Harold's 'brilliant move' with the linesman, reckoning it had turned the game as well as the chap's knee. Then Shirley astounded him with some informed remarks about the bloke who'd been marking Barry and how their defense hadn't adapted effectively when 'young Atkinson' had come on. Barry nodded slowly and appreciatively to this as Harold took a manly pull of his Double Diamond, then shared his experiences of Les the Lensman.

'Is he still getting about?' said Thommo scornfully. 'Crap he is, swore blind he'd got a picture of me getting clobbered by that Herbert from Hartlepool and that we'd have a case. When he did the films the picture showed me doing him – Hampson it was, crafty beggar caught me a beauty later on but naturally soft Les missed that.'

'So he clobbered you because you'd kicked him? said Shirley.

'Yeah, vicious bastard,' said Thommo and rubbed his gammy knee. 'Still playing apparently, monkey-hanging twat.'

Barry smiled. 'Saw him the other week as a matter of fact, asked after you. Gave away a ridiculous penalty.'

'I heard about that that,' said Harold keenly. 'That young player scored, then there was a proper set-to.'

'Just handbag stuff,' said Barry. 'Not like in Thommo's day.'

His mate lifted his chin a fraction and smiled. 'Is that the kid that came on today, Baz?'

'Yeah he's good, but Mullins wants to save him for next season if we get up.'

'Do you reckon you'll do it, does the club want to?' Thommo asked his friend.

Barry hesitated then said. 'Yeah, yeah I think so.'

Harold felt shocked to hear this kind of talk. Didn't a team always want to win, to play at a higher level? He reframed this a bit more diplomatically and was answered with knowing smiles and the insight that football clubs were complicated places. 'The Chairman's all right you know,' said Barry. 'Anyway, let's drink up it's a bit of a drive.' Harold remembered his secret commission and felt for the camera bag between his knees.

He and Shirley were let into the van through its back door to make themselves as comfortable as they could amongst old material and some ropes. In the front of the vehicle the two men of football talked with their insider's nous of transfer fees, compensation claims and something called 'aranbee'. Harold heard them laugh when Bob Guthrie's name came up. Soon the smell of petrol and the gassy aftertaste of keg bitter combined to make him feel queasy. He wished he were back at the house with Graham prattling on about Picasso.

Their journey seemed to take ages, but when he got out he began to benefit from what he took to be fresh sea air. Thommo had also given him a tablet to settle him down and he was beginning to feel a bit more like a night out. He picked out another dingy-looking pub in the distance and was told this was The Rocking Robin, their destination. When they got there he saw that it was clearly signed as The Gypsies' Tent but didn't say anything. Barry and Shirley went into the bar but Thommo went off somewhere and came back struggling with an amplifier. Harold decided to help him and was soon running up and down stairs with equipment including the various parts of a drum kit. He'd often fancied playing the drums and, when the drummer arrived to put his kit together, Harold stayed to ask him questions and tell him all about his photographic ambitions. The drummer got fed up with only being able to give half an answer before Harold fired off another one and told him he could have a go if he liked while he had a word with someone downstairs. Harold hammered away with the drumsticks, managing to work up a rough shuffle rhythm like Ginger Baker's and had a go at singing along, hollering out 'don't take the wrong direction passing through!' After a while he stopped and went back down to the bar.

He found Shirley in a corner with Thommo who asked him how his belly was. 'Much better thanks mate,' he said.

'Well have another one of these just to be on the safe side. Wash it down with some of the house cider, eh?' advised Thommo, and went up to the bar.

Shirley looked at him. 'What have you been doing, you're sweating like a pig?'

'Helping the band get set up.'

Thommo brought their drinks over. 'House cider for the young sir and house white for the young lady.' Shirley asked him about the wine. 'It's a special blend of Muscatel and Hock called Muck. The cider's called Piss by the way.'

'You what?' bawled Harold.

'Yeah, so when it's your round go up and ask for a Piss.'

Shirley held up a cautionary hand in Thommo's direction and told Harold someone was taking it. He laughed and drank some of his cider with the second pill. Then Barry reappeared and Harold remembered his brief from Mr Burleson. 'Do you think it'll be all right to take some pictures tonight?' he asked.

Thommo nodded and said it was a good idea as the band would want some, then sloped off to collect Harold's bag from the van.

Barry asked Shirley if she'd enjoyed the game. 'God yes, Eunice helped me to see what was happening. We all cheered when you hit the bar then when Harold nobbled the linesman...'

'It was an accident,' he moaned.

'Course it was,' said Barry. 'But well timed, they went to pot after that – what a day though eh, it's a special result when bonkers Bob Guthrie nets the winner.'

'Eunice said the young lad made the goal.'

'He did,' agreed Barry. 'He'll need some looking after in this league, he was up against a nice full back today – it'll be a different story in the next match.'

'Why?' asked Harold.

'York City at their place, they've got a pair of Frankensteins at the back – Cousins and Light. I played against them in the cup last season, I reckon they were built to order at the local railway works, rough as anything. I think even Big Bill would hesitate and he'll be out injured for the rest of the season anyway now. Coach Peacock'll have to dream something up for this one.'

'Maybe some of Thommo's tablets,' said Shirley quietly to him. He laughed, then his mate returned with the bag and swung it over to Harold who was beating out a loud tattoo on the table with his fingers. He caught it then stood up decisively saying he was 'off to take pictures'. Thommo shook his head gently and went to talk to the barman.

'So,' said Barry. 'You think you could become a football fan?'

Harold never did remember much about his big night out after he left the bar, intent on documenting an obscure rhythm and blues combo from Harlow. He later found evidence that beyond three unfocussed images of a beer mat he must have changed his mind. Then there was a fugitive and fading afterthought of playing the drums again, only this time before an audience who laughed and shouted. He was also pretty sure that he must have come to blows at some point given the black eye and swollen knee he felt when he came round next day in the back of Thommo's van. He took a while to locate himself as he had been covered with some old sacking and given Shirley's jacket for a pillow. He managed to get into a twitching half-sleep as the light began to ooze through the mucky window, but his head hurt and he felt very unhappy. He dreamed about furious football referees making him drink stale pee then woke again with a start and fretted about his camera bag.

'Okay mate?' said Thommo as he flopped into the driver's seat and scrabbled about for something.

'Yeah... yeah fine thanks. Erm... you haven't seen my bag have you?'

'Back at the 'ouse mate. The others are on their way.'

Thommo's terse replies had been enough to hint at another part of the evening. A part he'd decided not to think about so far. Well, he reflected, she was old enough to smoke and knew all about Eastern Europe – she should be able to look out for herself in Essex. With a cockney barrow boy he was supposed to be taking the interest in. He sank back into his bed of oily sacking and breathed in the lost, girly smell of her flying jacket.

Thommo suggested he get some fresh air and a stretch before they drove back. He eased himself out of the back of the van and walked up and down a short street patterned with bird shit opposite a long warehouse. Round the corner he could see the place where they'd been last night. It looked incredibly tatty all locked up in the grey light, like an abandoned chapel, somewhere the rats avoided. It was no wonder people waited till it was dark before they visited the place. Thommo came and stood beside him. 'Not quite The Winter Gardens is it?' he said.

'What was that band called, the one last night?' asked Harold.

'The Benfleet Flyovers – might put the old dump on the map, anyway, think on lad I need to get going soon. I'll drop you and Shirley at the station.'

She was waiting for them by the van, leaning against one side of it with her bottom and her feet braced against the kerb. She was thus able to lean forward from the waist to rock the vehicle slightly by flexing her legs. He felt that he didn't know her, he couldn't stop scratching either. She held up her hand and asked him how he was feeling.

'Awful.'

'Mmmm.'

'In we get,' said Thommo.

Shirley let herself into the passenger's seat so Harold had to muck in and make himself as comfortable as he could. Nobody mentioned Barry.

He had another scratch and winced at his headache, it was no good, it had been another daft idea. The other problem was that he couldn't remember much and wondered if this was why he felt so bad – and thirsty. As if reading his thoughts Thommo asked him if he wanted anything and stopped at a garage he knew would be open on a Sunday. After the garage man had filled up the van and nattered to Thommo for a bit he brought out a glass of water for Harold. He and Shirley hadn't exchanged a word while this happened and the rest of their journey to Southend passed in an awkward silence. He kept looking at her back, her hair was tousled and her shoulders looked cross. He wished that none of this had happened, he knew that the pictures he'd taken yesterday were all crap and he didn't care that Northtown had won – it all seemed silly and pointless.

Thommo pulled over by the station and let them out, giving Harold a smirk and wink. Shirley hung back for a few words with him leaning into the van with her bottom in the air. This was hard on Harold, he'd often fiddled with himself at night to pictures in his mind of Sandie Shaw or Clodagh Rodgers, but more recently they'd been shoved aside by Shirley's shapely form. He didn't want to consider what she had got up to with Barry Hutchinson. Thommo's van took off with a fart and she came over to put an arm through his.

'Well, what an adventure,' she said brightly.

'Yee, erm, yeah.' Harold's voice had taken refuge somewhere at the back of his throat. 'It's a shame it's such a drab day, though.'

She laughed easily and squeezed his arm. 'You're a nice bloke Harry – I'm sorry about last night, how are you feeling?'

'Rough, that cider I suppose. Look Shirley, how are we supposed to get home? I've got ten bob left – I knew we should have gone back with the others. I didn't really like Southend.'

'Don't worry, Barry's given us money for the fare back. He said it was the least he could do after our big night out.'

'Oh right, well, good enough eh?'

Shirley let go and began to run a finger down the printed timetable. 'Right, we need to get to Kings Cross then catch the London to Scotland mainline train. There should be a train in here now – yes, over there.'

There wasn't much to see out of his window but the warmth and movement began to lift Harold's spirits. Shirley was reading a magazine she'd bought and by the time they reached Liverpool Street he felt much better, and there was the Underground to come. He followed Shirley's example with the timetables and this also helped him to feel less of a nit. 'There's a train north at twelve fifteen then the next one, which is the last one, leaves at three twenty-five.'

'Well it's eleven now,' she said. 'Let's do something then catch the later one, I don't feel like rushing, do you?'

'No, not really. What do you fancy doing?'

'You decide.'

'Okay let's go to Trafalgar Square then have a look in the National Gallery.'

'Good idea Harry.'

He'd loved the Underground ever since an incredible childhood treat when his father had taken him to see Guy the Gorilla. It had resonated for him with some of the stranger aspects of Rupert Bear, his main window at the time on the collective unconscious and the smell as he and Shirley clacked along the platform acted on him like a Madeleine biscuit. Guy the Gorilla had been a bit of a let-down, he'd skulked around his cage then fallen into a trance in the corner. Harold had wanted him to beat his chest but the best he'd got was a half-hearted scratch and sniff affair with his bottom. Shirley was looking at a poster advertising secretarial work, then she asked him if he had a shilling for some more cigarettes. He asked her how many she smoked.

'Dunno – as many as I feel like. Why don't you have one?' The train came in before he could decide what to do but he thought he might try one later.

Shirley seemed happy to be at Trafalgar Square, after she'd got him to take her picture with some pigeons she linked arms with him again as they strode up to the National Gallery. Once they'd got up all the stairs they were both too tired to do much serious viewing, so they found a comfortable seat facing Turner's hallucinatory impression of a steam train in the rain.

'What time did you say our train was?' asked Shirley.

'Twenty-five past three so we should get there by three, really.'

'All right Mr Station Master,' she said, and put her arm round his shoulder, pulling them closer together. This was one of two amazing things happening to him at once and, as they sat together, the fantastic vision conjured up by the painter merged with the warmth of his companion to grant him feelings a world away from Dougie Peacock or soap rub-downs. When he got a girlfriend he would pin up something by Turner over the mantelpiece. He was struggling to accept that it was the painter who was doing the most for him, Shirley having been seduced by Barry Hutchinson when he wasn't concentrating. He could see now that good painting was real art, that what he was looking at was in a different league from photography. In as much as he'd given the painter much thought, Harold had formed a general view of murky daubs with insufficient detail. As for Shirley he was getting more detail than enough and her wants were all too clear. She had two older men on the go already and now he seemed to be part of the arrangement. He decided to have that cigarette when they went back down to the Underground.

Their frail intimacy began to disperse somewhere beneath the Tottenham Court Road when she sat opposite him and complained of bellyache. At Kings Cross she visited the ladies while he went for the cigarettes. He had a good view from his place by the silver slot machine which allowed him to see quite a bit of the platform unobserved by the other travelers. He fished out his camera and began to compose as the figures and shapes caught the light coming through the roof over the left luggage office. After three exposures he panned around a wider area and noticed a child with a balloon and a woman with a dog, but they were on their way out of the illuminated area, some couples were sitting outside a shut-up buffet. He watched them for a while through his viewfinder, then recognised someone he knew among the group. It was Dougie and he was holding hands with Mrs Burleson, he also realised it had been them in the stand after the game. The couple beside them seemed to echo their movements then the boy and balloon wandered into the frame. Harold pressed his shutter when the boy was in between the couples. He ducked out of sight behind a column but when he looked back they were sat as before. Mrs Burleson was laughing at something.

'Harold, what on earth are you up to now?' asked Shirley.

'Eh, oh just finishing off this roll of film.'

'Well I've got the tickets so we'd better wait on the platform.'

'Let's not – have a cigarette, I'll have one with you. Just look at the way the light picks out figures as they move through a drea–'

'Harold for goodness' sake let's just get on our train, I've had enough of this.'

'Is it here yet – I don't think it is, you know?'

'No and that's why we need to be on the platform, twit face.'

'I don't want to go on the platform just yet.'

Shirley regarded him as would an older girl lumbered with her idiot nephew for the day and who'd reached the pin-sticking stage. 'You and I are going to fall out soon unless you tell me what's wrong. Is it that stuff Barry's friend gave you?'

'No, I wouldn't have thought so.'

'Well what then? We can't set up house on Kings Cross Station.'

'All right, but this is a secret right?'

'Yes Harold – tell me.'

'You know Dougie from the club – he's on the platform.'

Shirley gave a patient nod to her numbskull nephew and waited for more. 'He's holding hands with the chairman's wife and I'm in his bad books because of that accident with the linesman and...'

Shirley marched brazenly into the open and called 'Where?' to Harold who'd shrunk back behind his pillar. 'Christ,' she called. 'You're right – come here, you've got to get a picture of this.'

'I already have, just come back – look, is that our train coming in?'

Shirley turned back reluctantly. 'What do you think he'll do if he claps eyes on you?'

'I don't want to find out. Just hang back till we can see where they get on.'

Shirley laughed but stayed put and they eventually saw Dougie and Anita get on at the top end of the train. Harold found Shirley and himself a compartment near the end. As they pulled out past Highbury Stadium, she lit up and passed the cigarette to Harold.

'Junior Reds' Supporters Club, Bootham Crescent, October 1983.

CHAPTER SIX

THE BALLAD OF TOM BURLESON

Dougie shifted in his seat and looked out onto the station platform. A little dog was scampering after a red balloon which suddenly lifted up and off through the light to the top of the station where the pigeons perched. 'I reckon Bill Thompson could help us there,' he said.

Anita frowned at him. 'Tom says he's a bloody fool, how is he going to help things?'

'Big Bill's not as daft as he seems – just getting a bit old for this game, that's all.'

She couldn't see how the awful Thompson would be of any use to them and their need for concealment but, as Dougie had shown, such an artful hand in things so far she was prepared to listen. Besides, if this weekend had shown her anything it was that she had fallen deeply for Dougie and that they must be together. 'Bill took a nasty knock yesterday, didn't he?'

'Aye, very nasty and that's where he can help us.'

'Go on.'

'Right, well it was all pandemonium after the game right? Folk going off in all directions, a right Fred Karnos and the police keen to get the coaches on their way back up north.'

'Yes that's right, I spotted Barry with that nice young lady...'

'Aye like as not – anyway, it's quite likely that Mullins said, or that I might have thought he said, better come Doug, Bill's in a bad way, you know, to the hospital like. So I followed on you see and there wasn't time to tell anybody.'

'Where do I come in, then?'

'Well Bill was so distraught and confused that he needed a woman's touch and as you were about at the time...'

'But I wasn't – you and me were canoodling up in that draughty bloomin' stand, weren't we?'

'Yes but Tom doesn't know that – he was hobnobbing with their chairman, Feathers told me, and if there's any comeback he'll confirm my story.'

'What about Big Bill?'

'What about him? He won't remember if he was on this earth or Fuller's. Anything he comes out with... well, you said yourself Tom reckons he's a fool.'

'But what about Mr Mullins? Tom says he's a crafty beggar – could flog central heaters to Africa, he says.'

He laughed out loud at this and told her not to worry about 'Sinbad'. The tale as told by Dougie was that he and she were so concerned for the hapless clogger who seemed only to be aware of Anita's gentle touch that they accompanied the rescue party to Southend Infirmary. It had all turned out for the best of course, but the urgency had caused them to lose track of time so there had been nothing for it but to put up in the town and keep a weather eye out for Big Bill, should he need more support later on.

'Yes, but Earl's Court is quite a distance from the hospital', she pointed out.

'Look, just trust me. It won't come to anything – if we're not careful the club's going to win promotion, your Tom will have enough to think about over the coming weeks, don't you worry.'

She looked at him and felt pleased with her canny lover; he was many sided and funny, had looked after himself in a way that men of his age seldom did. She knew the players looked up to him and when he wore his cap at a jaunty angle he resembled a slightly taller James Cagney. Tom admired him too, which seemed to make it all right. The place he'd taken her to the previous night had been a bit odd, though. She'd been promised dancing to a live orchestra but instead they'd had to sit in the dark listening to the most awful racket. 'That Bonny Scotts club was an experience, I didn't get any of his jokes. Why is a jazz musician someone who never plays the same note once? I don't understand.'

'Aye, a bit like the music – still it takes all sorts but I don't suppose London ways would go down well at Rice Carr Social Club.'

'Doug, pet, this whole palaver must have been expensive you must let me...'

'Don't worry about that now. I might be due a pay rise soon.' He laughed again and patted the seat next to him.

After Shirley left Barry rolled over to doze for a while in their seedy love nest at The Excelsior B&B. He'd thought northern girls were generally rough and ready but she'd been neither and not inclined to hide her disappointment when the train had come in ahead of time at Waterloo. As he reflected he realised that this made a difference; it had bothered him what she thought and her breezy way with him afterwards settled things; this wasn't the kind of girl he might encounter at Twinkles Night Club. He wanted to see her again, she was lovely and she'd shown a real interest in what a flat back four looked like. He'd never met a girl like her before.

Graham was lending a kindly ear to Harold's newfound enthusiasm for Turner over a late breakfast of cold beans and coffee made straight from their new boiler. 'The immensity of it all, I mean you wouldn't think it had been painted all those years ago. Bloody amazing.'

'Did you take many pictures yourself?' asked Graham.

'Yeah – one way and another. I should get them sorted out to show the chairman. He's taken quite an interest and it helps me to get access to the club. I really think I can make something happen with this project.'

'Where did you and Peacock stay in the end?'

'Oh, some tatty little place in Southend, The Seagulls or something. It wasn't very swish, Dougie said there was damp in his room.'

Tom Burleson sniffed and chopped his *Northern Scene* into a manageable shape by his plate. 'Well another time just try and phone or something, I'm not sure I like the every man for himself approach to the return journey.'

Anita let it go and waited for more, then he surprised her by asking if she'd noticed what had happened to Barry Hutchinson. 'I did actually, he was with that young lass who came with the photographer – I think they all went off together afterwards.'

He looked up at this. 'I need to see young Harold, there could be some interesting developments from that source.'

She wondered what he was on about but it seemed to be keeping him off the scent. 'Why were you concerned about Barry Hutchinson?'

'Why would anyone be concerned about Barry?'

Sod you, she thought, and went off to have a good crack at the bedding.

'So what happened to you then?' asked Mullins.

'Got caught up with something the chairman wanted seeing to. They all thought I'd gone along with you and Bill and went on without me. How is he?'

The manager looked at his coach for a second before replying. 'Bill? Oh, he'll be fine. You all right?'

'Don't worry about me.'

'Well things are getting exciting at this club, steady hands needed on deck and all, they say the slip of a lip can sink a ship. Keep your wellies handy, Dougie.'

He knows, thought Dougie, the bastard knows. Mullins knows everything, when Hutchinson's going to stray offside before he does it, when Leeds are going to come sniffing around after young Atkinson. He calculated that he wouldn't say anything to Burleson nor do anything to harm the promotion push but he was marking his card, reminding him what was important. No doubt he took a dim view of a woman on board a ship. Dougie watched Mullins saunter off down the corridor and imagined him in a three-cornered hat and silver buckled shoes, keeping his men in good order. He wanted to go for a nice natter with Kenneth but Reenie appeared in the corridor brandishing a can of Brasso. 'Dougie come here quick, you're wanted on the telephone.'

'What is it?'

'It's your lad, he's been taken bad.'

Dougie dashed to the office where Mrs Robson was holding the receiver. Reenie followed and stood in the doorway as he took the call. 'Yes that's right – when? – well where? – he's all right though? – how long? – well what on earth? – well didn't someone... oh right, yeah, yeah, but you say he's all right?'

Reenie looked across at Mrs Robson and mouthed something. The office manager looked at Dougie then mouthed something back from behind her hand. Reenie understood directly and nodded. 'Right,' said Dougie. 'I'll come straight away.' He put the phone down, thanked Mrs Robson then turned to Reenie. 'It's our Robert, he's had an accident at school – cracked ribs and a broken shoulder, poor lad'll be in a bad way. I'd best get over. Can you tell Boss Mullins while I nip home?'

'Is there anything we can do?' asked Mrs Robson.

'Look up the trains to Bolton, I'll come back before I go.'

'What happened?' asked Reenie.

'Fell down some stairs at school, something to do with a box of cleaning powders. They say he was out cold – I'd best nip.'

'Aye right,' said Reenie. 'Just mind on that bike.'

When he'd gone Mrs Robson asked her if there was anyone else they should notify, but Reenie thought that news would travel 'soon enough'.

As Dougie cycled home Harold was heading across to the other side of town wondering who he might tell at the art school about his drug-fuelled weekend with Shirley. In the end he confined himself to telling his tutor how close he'd been getting to his subjects.

'Mmm,' said Harolds tutor. 'Sounds as if it might be interesting – the dark room's free, I'll sign you in and you can get cracking. I'm free later on so we can have a look.'

The disciplined routines of the dark room had never interested Harold as much as inspiration of the moment. Some of his 'best shots' had been lost through sloppy and inattentive processing so he made a special effort to ensure he knew what went where. As he wound the films onto the developing spools he imagined the solid form of Mr Mullins standing by reminding him that winning efforts depended on painstaking approach work. Safely brought to negative form, he hung the films in the drying cupboard and set out his trays for the developer and fix in the 'wet area' by the sink. When the rolls were dry he carefully cut them into strips of six exposures and made contact sheets by laying six of these strips edge to edge on pieces of ten by eight-inch printing paper. When a sheet of clean glass was laid on top and the sheet exposed to the enlarger's light, it was developed to reveal six strips of positive images. Each sheet would hold around thirty-six pictures and Harold soon had his work ready for careful scrutiny. There were inevitably some rolls where more than thirty-six exposures had come out at the end of the roll and he was left with a few stragglers he knew he should contact for completeness' sake, but he couldn't be bothered and filed them away, sight unseen. He washed the printed sheets and hung them to dry.

Mrs Robson filed three letters and an invoice in the York City file, then turned to a smaller piece of paper holding a handwritten list of administrative tasks as Mr Mullins walked into the little office to ask for a brochure from a hotel near Heworth. She ran an efficient office and was able to produce it directly.

'I wish the first team were as reliable as you,' he said. 'You haven't seen Dougie have you? We're due to meet this morning.'

'He was in earlier, his son's had an accident and they've called for Dougie – he's in hospital.'

'The son?'

'Yes. Dougie's going across – he wants me to get him the train times. He looked badly shaken, he's gone on his bike.'

Mr Mullins took some time sorting out these details to his satisfaction then gave her a solemn nod. 'If he's got time tell him to have a word before he goes, and send the lad my best wishes if he hasn't.'

She watched him go. Bob Mullins had brought a real buzz to the place and liked to know what was going on ('run a tight ship'). She reflected that Dougie Peacock might do well to stay over at his son's for a while. She opened a window for Sailor the club cat and spotted the coach pedaling like the clappers past the cricket pitch with Kenneth in pursuit.

Anita had been pleasantly moved by Dougie's phone call, it could easily have been Tom who answered the call and even after she had taken in what he was telling her, Anita was able to build on the reality that she had been the first one he felt like phoning.

'How long will you be gone, pet?'

'Hard to say – depends how the lad is.'

'His girlfriend's there, isn't she?'

'Oh aye, but our Robert'll want to see me.'

'Yes, yes of course he will.'

'Anita, how was Tom about the weekend?'

'Fine – it all sounded right enough when I told him. He was more bothered about had I seen Barry Hutchinson and watch out for developments from that quarter. I don't get half of what he comes out with, these days.'

'Yes... anyway, I'll be gone at least one day and night so I don't know when I'll be able to phone. I'd best get going, Dot Robson's sorting out the train times for me.'

'Right... well, look after yourself, Eh?'

She replaced the receiver, then poured herself a sweet sherry and took it to the small conservatory. She wondered about the accident, reasoning that the knock on the head would either bring him to his senses over his dad and her or else render him senseless enough for it not to matter. Whatever the outcome this was an opportunity to be grasped, Dougie deserved some light in his life and she was determined to be the lady with the lamp.

Harold squinted at his contact prints. A number of them were overexposed and bleached, his tutor had seen this at once and wondered aloud whether it was worse to be able to process well but take poor pictures, or vice versa. 'You should keep light live,' he said. 'Also, remember that films that see the light never see the light of day.'

Yes, thought Harold, you've said that before. Terry took an interest in the impressionistic studies of Canvey Island but couldn't see where they might fit in with the rest. Harold drew his attention to the extended series from the dressing room and dugouts. This drew some thoughtful *mmms* and a 'potentially quite interesting'. High praise, and Harold cycled off home well pleased with his morning's work, ready to finish his essay on *Walker Evans and the Documentary Focus*. It was time to kick his drug habit and get down to some serious work.

The swiftest route from Northtown to Bolton as mapped by Mrs Robson took Dougie via York, where he had to change for Manchester. This meant he had twenty minutes to spare on his favourite railway station and he went up onto the main bridge to see what was happening; figures below moved through varied light, blokes in grey uniform pulled trolleys about, there were kids in caps and dogs yapping. He spotted an old lady taking directions in through an ear trumpet, then a party of pensioners appeared on the platform looking lost and distracted. She waived her brass thing in their direction and they moved towards her like ducklings. He felt pulled out of his own backwater but freer and less bothered than he thought he ought to be. Why wasn't he mulling over his affair with the chairman's wife or fretting about his son? Instead he found himself thinking about that kid with the camera, how much stuff there was to take pictures of from up on the bridge. Then he thought about the picture on the wall at home, how much Robert had missed his mum. Maybe this Anita business was best forgotten, he thought, for everyone's sake – even the teams – they'd need a result here next Saturday. His son was right, he was a selfish twat. Then he remembered last Saturday, how they'd made up after having to listen to a man fart through his trombone while his mate played the drums with a tablespoon. It had all been put right when they returned to their guesthouse at Kings Cross – Anita had made him feel he could crack eggs with a stick that night.

He shuffled away from his post on the bridge and bought a copy of the *Northern Scene*, the Manchester train was in so he boarded and made himself comfortable with the sports pages. Generally speaking it was a poor outlook for the region apart from Northtown's endeavours, so much was made of their late run for promotion and the 'splendid show' at Southend where much praise was heaped on 'messers Mullins and Peacocks masterly tactics' whereby 'the Shrimpers were sunk'. There was no mention of further funny business with a linesman but Dougie was unhappy with the picture of poor Bill Thompson out cold in the goal netting. This picture wasn't credited to Ernie Todd but his name cropped up elsewhere in a short piece promising a special feature on 'our conquering heroes' as part of the build-up to the big match at York on Saturday. Readers were advised to watch out for a photo special covering the lads 'on and off the field of play'. Dougie snorted and turned to the racing results as the train pulled out past the waterworks.

He came round as they pulled out of brilliant sunshine into Manchester Victoria. It took him a while to get his bearings then he remembered Robbie and his stomach turned. Anita seemed a long way off and he wished he'd had the gumption to get Reenie to travel with him. After another flap over his connection for Bolton he began to recover his composure and had a preliminary look at the *Scene*'s crossword. One of the clues asked him to locate the body part famously wounded in a battle and he thought again about the soft youth Tom Burleson was encouraging. The pair of them might need sorting out before too much longer.

Later that day Dougie sat by a hospital bed waiting for his son to see sense as Harold lounged in his deckchair by the fire,having spun some plausible stuff about Walker Evans; was he a poet with a plate camera? Did vernacular composition document truths? Someone had given him a reference by Gertrude Stein but it didn't seem to fit or make any sense. Anyway, he'd knocked out a couple of thousand words which, on top of his labours in the dark room, had left him feeling he was getting somewhere.

A smooth knock at the front door brought him round from this reverie. He was surprised to find Mr Burleson standing outside beside his car. 'Are you busy?' he asked.

'Oh I've just knocked off,' said Harold. 'Do you want to come in?'

'Yes – I want to know how you're getting on.'

'Well I can show you some work if you want.' Harold welcomed him in and passed over the contact sheets with the magnifier, then went off to put the kettle on and track down some Wagon Wheels. When he returned with the refreshments

Mr Burleson was holding one of the sheets near to the light and screwing up his eye.

'These are very good,' he said. 'You took these at that place where we stopped on the way down. This is just the kind of thing I was hoping to see – there's so much more to the life of a footballer than kicking a ball. Yes, you've caught Barry very well here.'

Harold drew his attention to the dressing room series and some of the crowd scenes. Mr Burleson was very complementary and lit up a cigarette. He also told Harold to call him Tom and held out his packet of Piccadilly. The silver paper seemed to smile and Harold caught the delicious whiff of fresh tobacco. He was puffing away like a veteran when Shirley came in. 'Hallo,' said Tom and stood up. 'We've just been going through Harold's pictures. What do you think of this one of you with my wife and Barry Hutchinson – very good don't you think?'

Shirley was caught off balance and frowned as he pointed out the image on the sheet. 'Look there, Barry's making you both laugh. Can you recall where it was?'

She looked at Harold and said, 'No not really – it might have been Harold making me laugh.'

Mr Burleson appeared not to hear and had another look. 'Oh yes,' he said to himself. 'Quite the character is young Barrington.'

She glanced at Harold again then went upstairs. He stubbed out his Piccadilly and sat while Tom made another close reading of the contacts. He eventually put them aside and asked Harold how the new water heater was 'shaping up'.

'Fine, it's made a real difference thanks, we can–'

'Now young man, I can see you know your business and I think what would help us all is a work in progress – generate some wider interest and get things moving. What do you say?'

'How do you mean?'

Tom continued in man-of-business mode explaining that his pal Ernie Todd was scheduling a big match special for Friday's *Northern Scene* which would be illustrated by images of 'the lads' at work and rest. 'Your material would be ideal, I'd make sure you got paid and credited – proper rates and all.'

'Well,' said Harold. 'Yeah, absolutely but I'm not sure I could get the prints made in time for Friday.'

'Oh, Todd will see to that down at their dark room. You can have the prints afterwards – Ernie's a handy man to know.'

'Right, well okay – you'd better take the negatives with you.'

'Righto, Ernie will look after them.'

Harold went up to the room he shared with Graham to fetch the film. Shirley's door across the landing looked very shut. He passed the negatives over in a large envelope with a cardboard back. 'Right there you are, the numbers will correspond to the prints on the sheets.' He pulled out one of the cellophane files to show Tom but it was the one with the tail-enders he hadn't bothered with, so he slid them back and found a full set. Tom looked at the film and chuckled, then put all the material in the envelope and tapped it lightly.

'Excellent, well I'll get off – watch out for Friday's *Scene*.'

The doctor Dougie talked to explained that Robert had actually taken quite a knock but it had registered on the harder part of his skull. He was still unconscious, though out of the woods and the longer he could sleep the better it would be. He was quite welcome to sit by the bed. Dougie sat as quietly as he could but soon exhausted what interest he could find in the

Formica trolley on wheels and the bland blue hospital decor. He finally focused on his son and thought about the little boy who'd asked him if Pontius Pilate had an aeroplane and used to sing along to *The Billy Cotton Bandshow*. He was therefore in a suitably moistened and reflective state when another figure sidled into the room. It was Karen, the girlfriend. She rested a hand on his shoulder and indicated with a graceful toss of her hair that they might step outside. He remembered her as a nice enough lass but, like the one who'd palled up with Anita on the way to Southend, would be all the better for a hairdo, and why did they have to wear jeans like the lads? She smiled and he saw that she was pretty, with sparkly blue eyes and a neat little nose.

'There's a visitor's room,' she said once they were in the corridor. 'I'll see if I can get us a cup of tea.'

Inside the sparse room an old woman was minding a baby who ceased squalling the minute Dougie sat down and stared at his grey cap. Dougie nodded to the woman and hoped Karen would be quick with that tea. She came back soon but empty handed. He told her not to mind.

'I could have done with one,' she said. 'What time did you get here?'

'Not long before you – got the first train as soon as I heard.'

'Team are doing well,' she said brightly. 'We always look.'

'Aye well, team can look after itself.'

Karen smiled at the baby and chatted easily with the old woman in a way he knew Anita would have done. She managed to find out why she was there (daughter having an operation) and where the baby's (Linda's) father was (night shift). Dougie piped up and explained that 'our kid' was in 'with a bang on the head' but was 'through the worst'. This made Karen cry so he moved closer and fished out a grubby hankie which he had the sense to put back when the old lady passed a tissue over from the baby's bag.

Dougie sat close enough for Karen to lean into his donkey jacket. After a while the lights came on and a nurse came in to fetch the baby and Granma. He couldn't tell from the nurse's expression how things might be, but knew this was the way they liked to deal with things and tried not to remember Linda. He had picked up quite a bit of how hospitals ran over the years through injured players – often with concussion – then there'd been that do with Robbie's mother. He understood why they hedged their bets, considered the worst outcome so that good news was a bonus if it came. Karen stirred when another family came in and began chatting.

'Where will you go tonight?' she asked.

He hadn't given this much thought beyond an image of bedside vigils beside starched linen and muttered a daft answer along the lines of not worrying about him.

'Well they'll not want us hanging about till all hours. You're very welcome to stay at ours.'

'Are you sure?'

'Of course, it's time you came.'

Then the doctor he'd spoken with earlier poked his head round the door and looked over to them.

As soon as Tom Burleson's smart car had motored away to the top of the street Shirley came downstairs. 'What did he want?' she asked.

'Some of my photographs, apparently they want them at the local paper for a picture special on Friday. Could be one of you in there with Mrs B and Barry – he wants me to feature Barry, you know.'

'Oh,' she said blandly. 'I'll tell him.'

Harold was feeling pleased and pushed his luck a bit. 'Are you and him going out then?'

'Well we're going out tonight if that's what you want to know – to Northtown's top bar and discotheque, The Cat's Whiskers.' The way she said this suggested that Barry was an unimaginative yobbo and Harold a nosey parker. He couldn't help wondering why she bothered if that was how she felt. He decided to wait until opening night at his first exhibition before he'd talk to her like that again.

'I'm sorry Harry, I'm not sure that we're going out properly. It's just that I've never really known anybody like him before, he's not like I thought he'd be.' She left it at that and he asked her what Graham was doing. 'Out sketching the Town Clock.' This prompted Harold to set about some more creative activity and Shirley went through to the kitchen and out by the back door.

'I just wanted to let you know it looks like he's about to wake up – we really could have done with him staying under for a bit longer but at least he can give us an idea what's happening when he's able to talk.'

They followed the doctor back into the side room where a nurse was bent over Robert. She stood back and the doctor took her place, Dougie noticed him gently push his eyelid up with his thumb then shine a little torch. After a minute he said 'okay' and that they could stay as he was coming round. The nurse brought in another canvas and metal chair for Karen so she could hold Robert's hand. Dougie thought he might not wake up and rested his hands on the mattress, which seemed surprisingly hard. He told himself he'd give up Anita if only the lad would wake up.

All Anita knew was that Tom would be working late again and she was glad really. All the recent activity in her life after so much stillness had left her feeling lighter, full of possibilities and ready for her own promotion from the bottom division. Tom being out more also released her from his probings and daft comments; he'd been at it that morning, letting it be known that they would soon see the bigger picture and that things were developing very nicely, thank you. She'd bitten at this and been told that he would show her 'in good time'. He'd then flattened out his *Northern Scene* and bored her stiff with a full-length account of dog racing at Durham, adding some nonsense about a smooth-haired Essex being sought. When she called him a bloody fool, he'd simply got up and left without finishing his Sugar Puffs. As she recalled this small unpleasantness Anita poured herself another sherry and decided to get to the bottom of things when he came home. Nothing he'd said had anything to do with her or Dougie. She switched on *The Newcomers* because she knew it would annoy him but, by the time the back door woke her, a man in a trilby hat was telling a woman behind a counter that she'd have to come clean.

'Sorry dear, didn't mean to disturb you.' She saw him glance at the sherry glass.

'Tom listen... ooh, my leg's gone to sleep. Listen, Tommy we need to talk about something, something you were saying this morning about...'

'Yes, yes, just get my shoes off. Do you want another one of those?'

Though she did, badly, Anita didn't want him to see the bottle and made a great show of putting the kettle on. By the time she brought the tray through she was composed enough to listen with a proper concern to Tom's tale of Dougie's dash to Bolton. He added the detail that, from what he'd heard, things were not well between father and son. 'Troubles close to home are often the worst kind, don't you think?'

'Yes well, be that as it may, what were you getting at over breakfast – interesting developments in good time? What does it all mean, because I'm blowed if I know?'

She took a deep breath and sat back. He didn't reply immediately and produced the reinforced envelope. He pulled out the contact sheets and passed them across. Anita peered at the first lot, then put on her reading glasses and moved over to her usual chair by the standard lamp. As she scanned the second sheet she let out a laugh of recognition. 'These are from that lad on the Southend trip. I remember him getting me to pose with his friend and Hutchinson – he's caught her very well hasn't he?'

'Has he caught you and Mr Hutchinson would you say?'

'Well Barry looks all right, caught his engaging grin right enough. That reminds me, we met the oddest fellow down there, an old pal of Dougie Peacock's called Feathers, a proper Romany by all accounts...'

She hadn't looked up since his last question, so missed the glare he'd fixed on her. Anita was very interested and took her time looking through them all, commenting favourably while he seethed unnoticed. Eventually he snapped and stormed off to bed. Anita waited ten minutes then reached for the Tio Pepe.

'What's in a snowball?' asked Barry as Shirley took her first sip.

'I'm not sure, I think it's like eggnog with something fizzy. I used to be allowed it at Christmas when I was at home and got a taste for it. What's in your pint?'

'Not a lot of beer,' he laughed. 'I'm sure they water it here.'

'Well that's good, isn't it? You don't want to drink too much, won't it spoil your game?'

'Not really, as long as you watch yourself and train properly it's surprising what a healthy body can take. I've known very few footballers who didn't like a drink, top players too. I had a trial once at West Ham, Bobby Moore had a nice chat with me, do you know what he said to me?'

Shirley caught the words of a song in the background and said, 'Show me the way to Aston Villa?'

'Very funny. No, what the England skipper said was "always remember son, win or lose on the booze".'

'Is it the pressure? I mean I can see that it's all very exciting at the club right now, but don't some people end up in trouble with alcohol?'

'People end up in trouble with booze in all walks of life and to be honest it's not that pressured. Not with a decent management set-up – Mullins is one of the best gaffers I've worked for and his number two, Peacock, is first class for this division. You feel looked after. First thing the gaffer did after Saturday's game was take off to see Big Bill in hospital. That means a lot to the players – hey, that reminds me – Dougie had to rush off this morning to see his son. Bad fall by all accounts, I hope he's back for York this week.'

'You'd miss him then?'

'Oh he'd be missed all right,' said Barry smirking as he sipped his watery beer. Shirley nibbled at the cherry then asked him what he meant.

'Well it's hardly a secret anymore, but I don't think they know that.'

'Who? Know what?'

'Dougie and the chairman's wife.'

She nearly coughed her snowball back up. 'You're kidding – Mrs Burleson and him?'

'Always watch out for the quiet ones.'

'But what about him – the chairman? He must know, it's bound to come out.'

'You'd have thought so, chairman seems like an odd chap though. Len Fidler worked for him at one time and reckoned his main interest in life was gas boilers through the ages. Maybe that's where Dougie comes in, laying some pipe. You could say it was all bound to come out.'

Shirley couldn't help laughing and allowed Barry to rest a hand on her knee. She enjoyed listening to him tell of the life of a footballer and got him back onto why Dougie was good at his job. She also liked Barry's modesty, she knew he was good, a cut above the others and that he had to be brave to play up front where you got knocked about. It offset his barrow boy cheek that seemed to go over well with older ladies like Mrs Burleson. She had done a few sketches of him playing from memory and thought she might ask if she could paint him if things went well.

They got up to dance, Shirley shadowing loosely his easy movements in a way she'd learned how to do. It was a small space but people managed to jig about happily enough without bumping anyone unless they wanted to. The record they were dancing to was by a band she liked and the song went 'ha ha said the clown' then 'in a whirl see a girl' which made her laugh because Barry liked to call her Shirl. There was another fast one on next and he smiled while she experimented with a hair-tossing manoeuvre, then Cilla Black came on singing through her nose about a world without love or any other kind of harmony as far as Shirley could tell, but it enabled them to smooch and snog for three minutes. 'I really love Cilla,' he said as they disengaged. Well, she thought, it would be a funny old world and led him back to a corner seat where they kissed for a while, then he bought her another snowball before walking her home. As they reached the back gate he asked her if she would be travelling to the York game?

'I'm not sure,' she said, and drew him towards her. In the moonlight the cobblestones glistened dully and a thin cat flattened itself along the gutter. Barry held her for a bit then pulled away. 'Save yourself for Saturday,' she said demurely.

'Yes,' he laughed. 'I fancy their number five.'

'Listen Barry, it might be difficult to get on Saturday, so if I can't will you get in touch next week?'

'Of course I will,' he said, and headed off up the lane. She watched him go and was able to notice Ambrose pass him at the corner as he came down with Glaxo on his lead.

'Was that Barry Hutchinson?' he asked wonderingly as he came nearer.

'Yes, I think it was,' she said, and went in.

CHAPTER SEVEN
KNOWING ME KNOWING YOU

'We should get it delivered really, now that they've poached you from *The Sunday Times*. I also think you should warn Mr Thompson that you're planning a series on local landlords letting out dangerous kitchens – he'd offer to pay our paper bill just to keep you quiet.'

'I dunno Graham, it's all small stuff really but it'll mark my card at the club. Mr Peacock will have to take me seriously; anyway I'll get a few copies, send one home.'

'Is there anything else you want from the shop?'

'Blue Riband would be nice – you know, celebrate.'

As he passed out into the back lane he heard Ambrose's mother singing a Methodist hymn, then Glaxo snorted from beneath the gate so he jogged up to Enid Street where the corner shop and newsagent showed him the way down to Green Park. Some spud-faced kids were throwing stones at an old man pushing a pram full of wood. The man said 'bugger off' and they ran laughing towards Harold. It was all he could do to stop himself ruffling fondly their tousled hair. Maybe he'd come back later with his camera, opportunities seemed to be falling into his lap these days and, as he knew, documentary photography with its neutrality and nuanced glance was so well placed to catch moments like these. The moments between moments where we could see what we were. There was a fresh pile of the *Scene* on the counter and Harold wondered how many people would look at it throughout the day. As the young woman in front of him paid for her Melody *Maker* and ten Park Drive he grabbed three copies of the paper, a Blue Riband and a Milky Bar.

Outside she had opened out her *Melody Maker* and lit up. He stood nearby and opened his own paper on the back page. There was a picture of Bill Thompson and mention of his slow recovery from 'perilous injury', then a larger piece on Middlesborough's upcoming game with Southampton – 'a real North and South story' – then he spied a note alerting readers that more Northtown news could be found inside the back page. And there it was, a whole page photo-special by 'young photographer Harold Hare' whose connections with a noted Sunday paper had brought him to the attentions of 'our own Ernest Todd' who had generously offered to showcase his work ahead of Saturday's clash with York City. By printing them small they'd managed to use twelve of his pictures set out in a rough chronology of a day at the club. Harold was thrilled to bits and breathed in the seductive taste of a fresh Parkie. He decided to try his luck. 'Anything good in yours?'

She looked at him blankly, her hair was piled in an unruly beehive and she squinted as she sucked on her cigarette. When she spoke her local voice sounded harsh and unfeminine. 'Nowt much,' she said, and gave him a tired smirk.

He thought she was beautiful though, like one of Walker Evans's overworked farmers. He wanted to pose her against a flat wooden background, catch the dignity and poise beneath the surface. 'Owt in yours?' she asked.

'Oh, something about the football team – quite interesting actually, some photographs.'

He was shaping to pass it over to her when she coughed and said, 'Somebody's wasting their film. Me dad sez they've done nowt yet.'

'They're doing very well you know,' he said feeling like a twit. She sloped off in her flip-flops before he could tell her about the beat scene on Canvey Island.

Graham had made the tea and was ready to have a look when Harold got back.

They laid the page down flat on the kitchen table. 'Hey, not bad eh?' he said.

Harold was pleased they'd used some of his best shots from the dressing room and dugout area with some of the actual match then one he'd taken at the roadside cafe and some of the training. He also recognised a stray picture of "coach Peacock" with Mrs Burleson on a station which he'd overlooked but which the paper had used. All part of the picture he thought and forgot about it till Graham pointed it out later. 'I like that one, all the stuff going on around them but they seem lost in each other. If you look carefully you can see they're holding hands.'

Harold looked more carefully and saw that his friend was right – it made a nice contrast with the ones of Dougie bawling from the dugout. He asked Graham where Shirley was then forgot about the picture again.

'I dunno, she went out yesterday and said she might be away for the weekend. Probably gone back home again.'

Anita watched her husband's car pull out into the town road. His last words to her to have a good read of the paper. He hadn't touched it and had seemed to make a point of leaving it unread by the kettle. She was becoming less bothered by the day with his mysterious carryings-on but still bridled at being told how to manage her day while he was away. Fridays *Northern*

Scene was left where he'd put it while she took on the kitchen cupboards, when they'd been put in good order she would have a crack at that pelmet, then reward herself by meeting Dulcie for lunch at Binns cafe. She'd just got the cleaning materials out from under the sink when the phone began to ring.

'Hello,' she said, flustered. 'Northtown 6521.'

'Ah thank goodness it's you,' said Duggie.

'Oh, it's you then,' she said.

'Yes,' he said. 'Me, not Walter Winterbottom or the Japanese Sandman.'

'You're taking a chance. What if Tom had answered?'

'Well I would have been Walter then – picking Sproates for the England team.'

'Are you all right, you sound pretty perky. How's Robert?'

'On the mend. They reckon he'll be fine. I've been staying at their place with Karen his young lady, it's ever so nice you know – they've got one of those coffee pot things you switch on at the wall. Very smart though I'm not much of a one for coffee meself like...'

Are all the men in my life going to pot? She thought. They were normally content to stay the same and were basically less trouble that way. Just hearing him like that made her itch for the known and settled attributes of a kitchen cupboard. 'So you and him have spoken then?'

'Oh yes of course, we've had a few words like.'

They must have been weighty nuggets by the sound of it.

'So you're talking again, that's good.'

'Aye but he's not to overdo things just yet, take things steady, things won't be the same for a while. He's maybe coming home tomorrow and I'm staying over for the weekend – have to miss the York match but there's more things in life than football especially as things stand.'

127

That's an awful lot of things for a man like Dougie, she thought, but was glad to hear he was happy. 'Listen pet, I'm so glad you and Robert have made it up but I'm thinking it's maybe you should have had the bang on the head.'

This brought forth a fond chuckle. 'You can clock me one as soon as I get back over. I'm really missing you, Nita.'

This subdued her mood a bit. 'Listen, Duggie, Tom's been very strange this past week and I don't know what it's about. I'm sure he's not cottoned on to us, but something's bothering him. He had me looking at some of that lad's pictures the other night, they're very good actually but I don't think that was his point. What do you make of it all?'

'Listen pet, it's difficult to talk now and I don't want to run up their phone bill. If I give you this number will you phone me here at four o'clock?'

'All right that should be okay, but if I don't it'll be because I can't, but I'll try later if so.'

He gave her the number. 'I'd best give Mullins a call next. Any news from the club?'

'I haven't heard much, as I say Tom's away with the fairies. This game tomorrow is important isn't it? I think I might have to go.'

'Yes it's very important and it would be a good idea to go, keep things normal like.'

'Normal like,' she exclaimed. 'Tell me what normal is round here and I'll do it – do you know what else he…?'

'Sorry pet I'll have to go, God bless, ring later.'

She put down the phone and smiled ruefully, remembering another time with Douglas. He'd shown her the scrapbook covering his playing days as a 'wily midfielder'. One report had dubbed him "slippery" and capable of reading a game "as might a chess player with calculating shrewdness". That got it about right and if he was a canny chess player then Tom was an erratic darts chucker whose missiles might go anywhere. Between them they would do for her one way or another. She went back into the kitchen and opened out the fresh newspaper, only to cast it aside when she read about the picture special on Northtown FC. She'd had enough, and went out early hoping she and Dulcie would find something else to talk about.

An emergency at Ferryhill Factors had taken up most of Tom Burleson's morning but it had brought in a big job that required his personal involvement. He'd been very taken up with this and the excitement had driven out all thoughts of errant wives and chancers from Chelmsford. It was two thirty by the time he'd had a wash and brush-up and he was running late for his important meeting with Mr Mullins to discuss the York game. He put his foot down from Ferryhill and arrived on time at three. 'Have you got today's *Scene*?,' he asked Mrs Robson. She had but feigned ignorance so he went off to find Eunice or Reenie but they had finished early and were with a third party in the back room of The Slaters Arms discussing the contents on their own copy. He looked about the boot room in vain, then Mr Mullins came in so he asked him if he'd seen it.

'Not in here, I think there's a copy in my office though. Come along anyway, I'll ask Mrs Robson to make us some tea. I heard about that slap up at Ferryhill – big job on there, eh?'

'Aye,' said Tom, feeling happier on familiar ground. 'Have to send off to Germany for some parts.'

'Really? Well at least we won't have to send off for a new centre half. Big Bill's out for the season now but young Podd's done well in the second team. I'm putting him in for Saturday.'

Tom nodded with his best man-to-man face, but his mind was elsewhere. He had to make a real effort to keep his end up for the next forty minutes as Mr Mullins went on about the York match, Big Bill's backache and sundry soccer matters he had only a passing knowledge of. He was sure Mullins knew this. When he'd decided their meeting was over Mr Mullins Handed him the paper saying, 'You'll be wanting to read this I expect, all very fascinating.' Tom took it to the boot room and shut the door.

Over at The Slaters Arms the landlord had made the back room a private party and joined the ladies to see what was in the paper. Reenie's other friend Greta was very affected by what was coming out and declared that she would 'go to France' over Dougie's doings while Eunice was rehashing a well-worn line on 'how Lady Bottomley was no better than she should be' which, although nobody ever really understood it, usually went down well.

'What's the crack then ladies?' asked Alf the landlord.

'Can we have another drink?' replied Greta.

'Aye go on – three halves of Strongarm is it?'

'Yes,' said Eunice. 'And some of your finest pickled eggs mine host.'

Alf furnished the refreshments and joined the party. After the pickled eggs had been polished off and fresh cigarettes doled out Eunice passed him the paper and asked him what he thought. 'Aye,' he said after due consideration. 'It's your lot over at the club – I'm a fishing man meself. Maybes a bit of cricket in the summer...'

'Yes,' said Reenie impatiently. 'But what about that one there?' and directed him to the final frame of the picture special.

Alf Smith was a steady, slightly ponderous man with the crinkled look of an unhurried cattle judge. After a close look he said, 'Why, it's a man and woman sitting on a railway station.'

'Yes Alf,' said Reenie. 'But not just any man and woman – look closely and they're holding hands. You wait till this goes up.'

Her two friends nodded and quaffed their beer. Alf fished out his glasses and took more time with the image. After five minutes of intense scrutiny he felt able to take a view. 'Now I reckon I know her.'

'Go on,' said Reenie.

He took off his glasses, laid aside the paper and said, 'Got it – Mrs Burleson. I've met her at a Trades Council do; her husband is a big noise there. But that's not him in the picture, that's not Mr Burleson the boiler man.'

'No,' said Greta. 'That's Dougie Peacock the lower league Lothario, a strutting Peacock, a seducer in flagranty.'

'You've lost me now,' he said.

Greta had been swinging her foot with some force as she'd cried up this last bit and took herself off to the ladies as soon as she'd finished.

'Greta knew him when they were younger,' said Eunice.

'So,' Alf said. 'This Peacock fellow is holding this lady's hand on a railway station...'

'Kings Cross railway station,' put in Reenie sharply.

'Kings Cross then, well maybe she was lost or something and he was giving her a helping hand you might say.'

'Alf Smith are you soft or what, how many years have you been in the licensed trade? Take it from me, this is the goods and you heard it from us first.'

Alf stood up. 'Right, I'll bear that in mind at the next Trades do, should be one coming up soon. I'll just consult yon calendar.'

'There'll be no more la-de-dah councils for her,' Eunice called after him. 'Mind there'll be some comings up though.'

A flushed Greta rejoined them and the cackling set up in earnest. Alf left them to it; it wouldn't be long before opening time came round again.

The first Anita knew of the revealing photo-essay was roughly coincident with her husband's tormented pacing of the Northtown FC boot room where he was lost in a reverie from hell featuring disbelief, denial and Dougie Peacock. 'You've been a fool,' he wailed. A bloody fool to think it was Barry Hutchinson who no doubt had his pick of the scrubbers round the town and what did he imagine Anita would want from an ill bred yobbo such as he, anyway? But this, cuckolded by a bluff rough man of the playing fields who had barely a civil word for anyone. One who might keep pigeons and shoot rabbits holding hands with his Anita on a common railway platform in black and white for all the world and Northfield to see. All that eyewash she'd been giving him. He picked up a stray boot and hurled it at an old wardrobe at the far end of the room. It thumped against the wood and sheared off into a pile of netting. As Tom stared at the wardrobe door it began to creak open.

It hadn't really hit Anita at first. In fact she almost missed the most relevant image altogether, having seen most of them anyway; but the sight of Dougie caught her eye.

She felt as if she were falling through space like that chap who chases Bugs Bunny and ends up falling off a mountain and it takes him till halfway down before it dawns on him. Her reactions hit critical mass soon enough and the first casualty was Tommy, their ancient tabby who caught a direct hit from the flying paper as he slumbered blamelessly in his basket. He managed to drag himself upright to see if there was anything else coming, but Anita's bellicose wail got him going with as much speed as he could muster to a safe haven beneath the bed.

He was carried off permanently by a heart attack before he could get there and would be found later, behind the door of the spare bedroom.

After some milder and more focussed shrieking Anita poured herself a big drink and parked herself on the seat in the hall where she wept and stamped her feet. She'd been a bloody fool and now there'd be hell to pay and no mistake. She took a firm sip from her sherry and gradually composed herself. When she was sufficiently calm she found the number Dougie had given her and put through a call to Bolton. A young woman answered to tell her that Dougie was out buying a paper but shouldn't be long. This bothered her at first but she was able to reason that sales of the local paper might be sparse in Greater Manchester. Soon after this her phone went.

'Is that you?' he asked.

'Of course it is – you great birdbath.'

'What's up pet?'

'The game is, that's what.'

'What, the York match?'

'No you great dishcloth our match, our little game. It's all over the blasted paper, that's all.'

She heard him gasp. 'It never is – what's it say – what paper?'

'Today's *Northern Scene*, all in black and white, a picture spread for all to see. We've had it now. It's down to that daft ha'porth from the art college – I thought it was a bad idea you encouraging him...'

'Anita, slow down pet. What do you mean about a photo spread, what do you mean exactly – I mean what's in it?'

'As far as I can see it's mostly from that trip to Southend, you remember him taking pictures all over the place? Well, soft Ernie Todd's given him carte what sits with the back page. A look behind the scenes with our lads and we're in it, holding

133

each other's hands on blasted Kings Cross station. And Tom's in on all this too you know, been round to see the lad, asking me what I think of his efforts but I never spotted that one.

'What are we going to do Dougie? Tom'll be home soon – talk about *Candid Camera.*?

'The first thing I'm going to do is banjo that kid with his ruddy camera. What's he think he's playing at spying on us, do you think he's in Tom's pay?'

'Oh I don't know. Dougie what am I to do? It's all up for me, now. I'm sure Tom's gone daft, I don't know what he'll do next – in and out of the house like Piffy at all hours, laughing like Bella Lughosty…'

'Lugossi, Bella Lugossi – yes he's onto something but why hasn't he said anything outright? Anita – Nita are you still there?'

'Yes it's just come to me. Christ this gets worse – he didn't think it was you, he thought it was somebody else I was having an affair with, he thought it was Barry Hutchinson. It's crackers but it all makes sense now.'

'Thought it was Hutchie – thought it was you and him, has he gone soft or what?'

'Oh thank you Douglas, thank you very much. What do you think they'll say about you and I?'

'You know what I mean, pet. Anyway Hutchie's taken up with that lass come down to Southend with us. Very nice as I remember.'

'Hell's teeth man, are you taking any of this in – what are we going to do?'

He knew what worked best whenever she was getting her knickers in a twist, and puffed up his capable man-for-all-seasons front. 'Listen. I'll be back over as soon as I can but in the meantime I really think you should get out if you're worried aboutTom, and I agree you should be. Where could you go?'

'I don't know. Dulcie.'

This foxed him. 'Eh? Anita breathe deeply it's me, Dougie ...'

'Dulcie – I had lunch with her today. I'm off round there now.'

'Right, good. Phone me as soon as you get there.'

'Why did we have to go to Southend in the first place though? None of this would have happened if only...'

'We had to go. It was an away game.'

'Yes of course – howay the Shunters let's get things in perspective.'

'Listen, Robbie was still asking after you, we had a proper natter.'

'Well you'll have plenty to tell him now, I'm off.'

'Well take care – and ring me.'

Wring your neck, thought Anita, as she barged through the half-open door into the spare bedroom to find a suitcase. Dulcie Dorman lived on the other side of town but Anita wanted to get out as soon as she could. She managed to lug the case as far as the Travellers Rest down the road, where she phoned for a taxi. The early evening drinkers were all men and they looked her up and down as she ordered a sherry. On the bar looking well-thumbed was a copy of the *Northern Scene*. She took it with her when the man from Station Cabs turned up and had a closer look on the way over to her friend's house.

Although Anita's haste had been understandable Tom never did return to their house and was not in the party travelling to York the next day. Later on Kenneth the groundsman recalled seeing him getting into his car quite late on the Friday night with a box. He'd thought the chairman seemed preoccupied and that it was unusual to see him around the club office at that time. The night watchman at Burleson's Boilers reported a light on in the upstairs office over the weekend, but put it down to a sensible security measure.

Harold spent much of his week end taken up with the endless wonder of documentary photography: its subtle concern with bearing witness to the world, how it was like dust suspended marking the place where a story ended. Or began, who was to say? This, it seemed to him, was one of its magical taproots, how it could catch a moment in time which existed in parallel time, how an image might be orphaned from its object to grow a life of its own. But then again, who really 'owned' an image, the subject or the person catching the light? This pre-occupied Harold as he prepared his next assignment, then took up most of Sunday when he was pretending to be a train spotter in order to take some unobserved pictures of people waiting for connections. People lost in time. Lost to themselves even, caught in...

'I might have known it would be you,' sneered a familiar voice.

'Eh, oh hello Mr Peacock are you...?'

'About to knock your block off? Aye, but that can wait – it's time you and me had a little chat.' Harold stood still and remembered how the players behaved for the coach. He followed him off to a small shelter where he assumed he'd be set about at Mr Peacock's convenience. He wished he knew what he'd done.

'Have you any idea what you've done son?' asked Mr Peacock as soon as they were alone. Harold had heard that Northtown "had got beat" at York by a disputed penalty but couldn't see how he might be blamed. "You don't do you? Do you know where I've just been?'

Harold wished he'd ask him one he knew like how Cecil Beaton had managed to make the Blitz resemble a theatre set but he could see this was unlikely. 'To York haven't you, you must have stayed overnight – a bit of a disas–'

'Not to bloody York, I've been to Bolton to see my lad who fell down some stairs and was in a coma. Do you know what it's like to–'

'No, no I don't, I'm sorry but I don't and if you're trying to rough me up I wish you wouldn't. I don't know what all this is about, I'm just here minding my own business when you–'

'Ah well that's just it, isn't it? You're not minding your own business you're minding everybody else's. I've been watching you; do you think folk are daft? And as for plastering it all over the local paper, what sort of trick do you call that?'

Dougie was glaring at him and something told Harold that things might go better for him if he found his tongue. He also thought he knew why the older man was so angry. 'Well we thought a photo spread would catch people's attention, generate some interest and also give my work an airing. I do actually think some of the pictures from the Southend match came out well.'

By this point Dougie had decided he was dealing with a complete berk who merited sympathy rather than a good shake. He softened his approach. 'You said *we* thought, who else was involved in this caper?'

'Oh well, Mr Burleson came round and said he'd fix it with Mr Todd at the paper, all I did was hand over the negatives and permission for Mr Todd to print whichever pictures he liked. The rough idea was Northtown to Southend and back with our winning team.'

Dougie just looked at him, then said, 'So it was Ernie Todd who chose the pictures, but Tom was involved as well? You say he came to your house?'

'Mr Burleson? Yes, he's been before to fix our kitchen water boiler. We got talking then and he was very keen on my work. He wanted me to feature one of the players in particular.'

'Barry Hutchinson?'

'Yes that's right, how did you know?'

'Never mind,' said Dougie quietly as he looked out to the opposite platform. 'You like taking pictures on stations then?'

'Yes, it's something about the way time seems to–'

'Never mind that – do you remember taking some on Kings Cross station?'

'Yes,' said Harold. 'Yes, I do.'

'Aye well, it's them that's caused the trouble. Why on earth Toddy put that one in I'll never know.'

'The one of you and Mrs Burleson?'

'Why on earth did you take it?'

'I just liked the way you looked, together, with the setting and everything.'

Dougie didn't say anything and continued watching what was happening on the other platform. People were moving about and someone was shouting 'Hurry up!' Eventually he spoke, 'Well, why not just enjoy the view and let it go? There's pretty pictures all over the place, all the time you're pointing your camera one way you're missing something else.'

Harold could not come up with an answer to that. 'I'm sorry it's caused so much trouble.'

'Well it's all out now.' This was said quietly and Harold thought he saw the shadow of something like a smile play about Dougie's face.

'Is your son all right?'

'Aye, he'll do.'

'Shame about the result.'

'Could have been worse.'

'How do you mean?'

'Well, the other teams around us all slipped up so we can still win promotion if we beat Tranmere at home next Saturday.'

'Big match then.'

'Biggest for a few years. Need to be focussed for that one – you coming, son?'

'To the match.'

'Of course, got to immortalise us. Don't worry about this other business, it'll get sorted one way or another.'

Dougie gave him a playful punch in the stomach, then sauntered off into the timeless station light. Harold sat down to catch his breath, coach Peacock had really put the wind up him. No wonder the players didn't gave him much trouble.

After visiting Anita at her friend's Dougie decided to walk back to his own house, to let his thoughts settle. As he walked down the passage to his back door he hummed *Begin the Beguine*. Not far away a furtive presence lost itself in the trees.

CHAPTER EIGHT

THE PATH WITH A HEART

Monday morning bathed Northtown in spring light; blossom lined the gutter in Green Park where Glaxo uncoiled his early day motion and birds piped up their songs. Old stonework welcomed the sun and babies dozed in backyarded prams. Dougie Peacock felt like a new man who questioned why the world shouldn't know what was right and true; things were moving fast – and Northtown might win the Fourth Division. If it all came right he'd take Anita to Scarborough. He turned on the hot water and washed up his breakfast pots.

At the Northtown Stadium others said that 'Dougie'd done it now' by not only coming between man and wife but possibly jeopardising the team's big chance. 'Pair of daft beggars,' said Reenie.

'It's all round the doors,' said Eunice. 'Madam's gone to her friends and no one's seen Tom since Friday. Kenneth reckons he was over here late on, up to something.'

'Up to something?'

'Aye but Kenneth couldn't be sure – he said he'd get back to me.'

'Well, there's more to come there then.'

Reenie lit up a cigarette. 'Is love's young dream about yet?'

'Oh yes, spotted cycling round the cricket pitch whistling a happy tune.'

'Well that'll not last, but thank heavens Robert's all right.'

Eunice smiled tartly to the Vim canister. 'Anyway, what about our lot last Saturday? Talk on the terraces was that we were robbed but I'm not so sure – we're missing Big Bill and young Atkinson got chopped to pieces by their defense, they'd have thought twice if Thompson had been about.'

'York have always been a rough lot,' said Reenie. 'It's all that chocolate, goes to their heads. Still the lad'll have to take it if he's serious and he's got the ability – see that pass he sent Hutchy through with? Only the goalie to beat and he puts it wide.'

Eunice snorted. 'Yes well we know all about him, minds not on the game these days and fancy giving away that penalty – what on Earth was he doing faffing about like a bunch of grapes in defense? He should have been waiting for our midfield to play him in down the channels.'

'Well let's hope that Dougie's got his head right this morning. We need to focus this week; it all comes down to Tranmere. Is your bottle of doo-dah different to mine?'

Harold's day began much later. He'd lain awake for a long time trying to build up a version of events that he could live with. Particularly a perspective on documentary photography capable of screening out the doubts. He'd eventually fallen into a troubled slumber as the lights came up and managed to doze away most of the morning. His dreams brought little comfort; at some point he'd been feeling Mrs Burleson in the middle of a football pitch, both were naked and the grandstand was full; then Dougie ran out to punch him as the linesman waved his

141

flag. This shocked him awake and he found he was dying to piss but had a full erection. He managed to sort things out to his satisfaction and went downstairs where he found Shirley smoking coolly in the kitchen. He saw that she'd been working at a large drawing, something quite normal by her standards; not an abstract policeman in Grosvenor Square or a Vietnamese reading the news. It was a headless figure, male with smaller studies of him on the same page bending or running. The drawings were well executed and clearly based on Barry, a subject he knew to have meaning for the artist. He resembled a Greek god, a symbol of ideal masculinity, albeit capable of giving away soft penalties. 'That's really good,' he said and put the kettle on to boil.

'Hmmn,' she said. 'I'll leave it and have a look later before I decide.'

He made them a drink and they went through to the front room where she produced the previous Friday's *Northern Scene*. 'They've come out very well Harry, you must be pleased. You got me and Barry with Mrs Burleson well – we didn't know.'

'Yes well, that's the problem. Didn't know what I was doing did I? Look at that last one.'

'The one with Dougie and Anita?'

'Yes, you remember on Kings Cross station – I'd forgotten all about the bloody thing. Now it's all up in the air and I'm to blame.'

Shirley shrugged. 'It was bound to come out one way or another, apparently it's common knowledge at the club.'

'You what?'

'People know about it at the club. Barry told me.'

'Everybody knows? Did you know when I took that picture in London?'

'No, not then and not everybody knows – well they do, but ... you know what I mean. It wasn't exactly common knowledge. Mr Burleson didn't know and they didn't know it was known.'

'But they do now, the revelatory power of our local lensman eh?'

'Oh, I shouldn't worry Harry, besides it's a nice picture.'

'Dougie didn't seem to mind that much actually, not as much as I thought he was going to.'

'When did you see him?'

'I bumped into him on the station yesterday. He put the fear of God into me but he seemed to be in a good mood as well. His son had been ill but he's getting better. I don't understand really, he's an odd chap.'

'Barry says the players are very wary of him. He used to box at one time and apparently once decked Big Bill in a gentleman's disagreement after a game – they used to call him "Rowntree" because that's as far as most people would last with him.'

Harold remembered that playful punch on the station and how big Big Bill really was when you sat next to him in the dressing room. The silent world of men seemed impenetrable to him just then. Beyond the reach of all the lenses in Germany, the fatuous blatherings of art school pictorialists. 'What's your drawing of Shirl?'

'Something I just felt like doing, not part of my coursework or anything.' She picked up her large sketchpad and worked for a bit longer. He sipped his tea and watched, admiring her concentrated commitment. He asked her what Barry thought about the Tranmere game on Saturday.

'All I know is how keyed up they all are, I feel it as well. Are we going?'

'Yeah, of course. I don't think all this Dougie business will put them off, do you? I mean it shouldn't, do you think?'

'Well if it does it's not really your fault, is it?'

'No,' said Harold. 'Not really.'

Tom let himself into Dougie's yard by the back lane and his kitchen with his old army knife. He closed the door quietly behind him and laid his workbag down on the kitchen table. Smiling to himself as he sized up the ancient Bessemer by the sink he began to hum *Don't Jump off the Roof Dad (You'll Make a Hole in the Yard)* and made some rough estimations about explosive impact and carrying distance.

The first Harold heard of it was during teatime the next day. He'd spent most of Tuesday in college looking at Victorian portraiture and taking in a lecture on 'ways of seeing', so by the time he switched on Mike Neville he was ready for a nice nap,not the fright of his life. The popular newshound was wearing his gravest face as he intoned over some footage of a damaged rear entrance 'from Northtown where residents told of "an almighty explosion" around three thirty yesterday afternoon – I'm handing over to our local reporter who is at the site on Olympic Street at the west side of the town'. 'Our man from Northtown' was Harry Brown and he was able to give more details including the detail that 'the injured man was thought not to be the actual resident who is the well-known man of football, Dougie Peacock'. Harold fell into a panic and had trouble getting his bearings; was the injured man Dougie or not Dougie and if not Dougie, who? The best outcome would be damaged but not Dougie, and he went into a kind of vaporised swoon with the phrase stuck at the front of his head.

Graham appeared and Harold blurted out 'Dougie's not damaged!' then burst into tears before telling him he'd made something bad happen with a photograph and that he didn't want to be a documentarist if all it meant was damage. Graham rested a pensive hand on his pal's shoulder and wondered about that stuff Dutch Martin had been selling at the college. He'd already picked up something from Shirley about Harold's adventures on Canvey Island. He hoped it was that and not a peep around the bend. He took his time then asked Harold what had happened.

'Look it's on the flippin' telly, now.'

Graham looked as Mike Neville summed up the headlines and another picture of Dougie's damaged kitchen came on. 'Is this that explosion yesterday? I'm sure you haven't killed anyone with a photograph, Harry.'

'You know about it?'

'Yeah, it was in the paper this morning – "man found unconscious in dangerous kitchen".' He found their copy. 'Here, have a look.' Harold took a deep breath and read:

mystery surrounds the events thought to have taken place at the home of local sportsman, Dougie Peacock. He was not there at the time of the blast, being fully involved in preparing his charges for their vital game this week at the Northtown Stadium.

Harold calmed down a little. 'I haven't seen the *Scene* yet, no one reads it at the college – Dougie's definitely all right, what's it say?'

'Mr Peacock unavailable to comment.'

'But able to, if he wanted to?'

'Sounds like it. They're reluctant to name the injured party yet but some detail has emerged; there was evidence of tampering with the kitchen boiler and some houses have been evacuated. Northern Gas has sent in a crack team.'

'What do you think they mean by tampering?'

'Search me. Your mate who fixed ours would know. Maybe the gas team will consult him.'

'I've a funny feeling in my water about this,' said Eunice. 'There's something not ringing right.'

'Go on,' said Reenie.

'It's something Kenneth said.'

'Kenneth, what's that cloth head know about anything?'

'Something about a box and Tom Burleson last Friday. Late on, Kenneth said.'

'Phurpp,' said Reenie. 'It's maybes Kenneth got knocked on the head in Dougie's kitchen.'

Eunice sipped her barley wine judiciously and looked into the far corner of the snug. 'No Reen,' she said. 'I don't think it was Kenneth.'

Shirley and Barry had taken the train to Newcastle where he was treating her to a Berni Inn blowout complete with a bottle of red wine. 'When I told Thommo I was coming up here he took the pee, told me nothing ever happened north of Nottingham except flooding from the coast and sheep shagging.'

'That sounds more like Essex to me,' said Shirley quietly as she speared a soggy mushroom. 'Was he any good before his injury?'

'Not bad, lower league though. Had his chances, a scout came from Fulham once but nothing came of it.' Barry coughed nervously and pulled a little box from his jacket pocket. For one awkward moment she thought he might be about to produce a ring, but it passed and he knocked a couple of little pills into his hand and put them down with some wine. He noticed her raised eyebrow. 'Just to steady a few nerves before the big match. Giving that stupid penalty away hasn't helped.'

'All this business at Dougie's house won't help either, will it?'

'It might lift the pressure in a funny kind of way.'

'Well,' she said. 'It certainly lifted some pressure in Dougie's kitchen.'

'It is odd though. This mystery man; the police might want to talk to people, people at the club even. Nothing like this ever happened at Brentford.'

'Would you be able to come with her, sir? I think she might need someone there.'

Dougie looked at the young police constable and nodded. 'I'll just see if she's ready.'

Mrs Dorman's bungalow seemed to have a good few rooms,but the sound of repining voices drew him to a bedroom door near the back of the building. He stopped and found himself admiring the fitted carpet and taking in snatches of fraught conversation from Anita and her friend: 'should never have let it get this far' – 'but we don't know for certain' – 'it all makes sense now' – 'could have been a burglar' – 'poor Tommy' – 'but we don't know'. Then an impassioned sob from Anita and further 'what were we thinking' and 'blame myself'. The other voice had stopped and he knew that if she weren't diverted soon Anita would set up a Wailing Wall of her own in Dulcie Dorman's boudoir. He steeled himself and knocked. There was no answer but he sensed movement behind the door, then Dulcie put her head round, she seemed glad to see him.

'Anita,' he said as gently as he could. 'They want us to go now – I'll come with you then bring us back here eh?'

Mrs Dorman nodded encouragement and Anita emerged whey-faced and penitent. She allowed him to take her hand but wouldn't meet his eye and looked out of the police car window all the way to the hospital. It had been another fine day and, when they got there, the big building cast long shadows. A nurse coming off duty smiled to them as they parked. Dougie felt a complete pillock.

He opened the door to reception for her and she began to speak. 'They won't tell us anything. Why won't they tell us anything, Doug?'

'It's all very delicate I suppose, if it isn't him they'll have upset everyone for nothing. As far as I know he's unconscious but stable, whoever it is.'

The policeman took them down a long squeaky corridor where a young lady doctor met them at the far end and ushered Anita into a side room. Dougie squinted through the round window in the door but couldn't place the bandaged head of a figure connected to some tubes. The doctor was talking to Anita and showing her something in her hand, then she reached across to move some of the patient's dressing and he heard Anita cry out. He stood back shocked and the nice PC told him he'd best sit down and went off to sort out a cup of tea. Dougie had been badly shaken, but he was thinking of Robert and what might have happened. As for Tom Burleson, he'd never rated him much and now the daft devil had nearly blown himself up in his kitchen, what a performance. The policeman brought the tea. He could hear Anita sobbing.

By Wednesday the local press was able to give out more details and news spread. Mrs Robson had been busy with get well cards to sort out and even a bluff phone call from Hartlepool which she'd been asked to pass on. With demands for tickets for the big match and Dougie Peacock's low profile, she'd been busier than she could remember. However, she'd steadied the ship through rough passages before and she knew Mr Mullins would count on her. She set about the pie order estimating that an unusually large amount would be required, then young Atkinson appeared in the office asking for a couple of complementaries. He melted away when Mr Mullins' voice came through from the car park. The manager appeared looking awkward with fruit and flowers. She could tell he was out of his depth and found him a box. 'How's he doing?' she asked.

'Anita says he's off the danger list but he can't remember anything and spends a lot of time asleep. If you see Dougie tell him I want a word.'

Dougie was at that moment taking tea and sympathy in the boot room with two of the few people he could trust at such a time. 'What have I done Eunice? To think it should have come to this – Anita's in bits over it.'

'Aye well, as long as long as he's not it'll all get mended one way or 'tother.'

'He can't take in half of what she says, doesn't know where he is half the time.'

Eunice sniffed and turned her attention to a distant corner of the room where a discarded corner flag leaned against a flaky wardrobe. 'Did Kenneth say owt to you about boxes, Doug?'

'Eh? No, not as I can recall. Told me I wanted me head testing, even Kenneth can see that. What was I thinking?'

Reenie looked up from her newspaper. 'You were following the path with a heart.'

Eunice muttered something on her way to the wardrobe and Dougie asked her what she was 'on with now' in the manner of a man tried enough. 'It's here in the paper,' she said.

Dougie stood up and demanded to see what had been written on his account now. 'I'm nothing more than a laughing stock in this town as it is thanks to that blasted rag.'

'Sit down man, it's not you it's Carlos Castaneda, here look.'

'Carlos who? Has Mullins signed a Mexican now? The world's going daft.'

Reenie drew his attention to the back page of 't'*Scene*' where the build-up to Saturday's 'day of destiny with Tranmere' was gathering pace with an extended feature. Dougie read it through carefully then declared it 'utter tripe'. 'Who the blazes have they got writing us up these days? What's happened to Willie Wharburton, he might have been three sheets to the wind from The Boot and Shoe but at least you could understand him? He never quoted soft beggars with daft names, can you imagine our lot if Mullins told them to follow the path to enlightenment? Do they think Thompson was following his heart when he clattered that kid from Hartlepool? Who is Simon Snaith and what sort of a name does he think that is anyway? I've never read such piffle in the sports section of a respectable newspaper.'

Eunice piped up from the wardrobe. 'He's from the college, some sort of work fellowship, probably knows your young friend. The readers reckon he's brought us luck so they're keeping him on for a bit longer. Besides, Willie's in for another rest cure and it could be a long job this time.'

'I'll be joining him at this rate,' said Dougie.

Outside the boot room Mrs Robson could be heard asking someone if they'd seen Mr Peacock. Reenie looked at him inquiringly but he shook his head gently and the voices faded away. He turned to the local news pages but there was nothing beyond a note that the gas was back on at Olympic Street and a local man was helping police. He took a deep breath and put the paper down. Reenie had joined her friend by the wardrobe of mystery, which had offered up a pile of treasures now available for inspection on the table by the sink. Reenie rummaged and found a catering pack of paper doilies ('told you they'd turn up'), some Christmas decorations, several pre-War football shirts and a bag of cement which Dougie manhandled gallantly into the middle of the room for Kenneth to see to.

'Eee,' said Reenie. 'Look here now.' The other two looked at her. 'It's a box. A carefully hidden box if I'm any judge, and remember what Kenneth said.'

After a pause Dougie told her to leave the money and open the box. Eunice brought it out carefully, it was an old shoebox and surprisingly heavy. They stood back to let Dougie dip inside and bring out a variety of wires, screws and odd-looking clasps. At the bottom he found a small solid object shaped into a rough sphere wrapped in dark heavy paper. He set it apart from the rest of the stuff and pulled a knowing face.

'What is it?' asked Eunice.

'A crow scarer,' he said.

'A what?' said Reenie.

'A small explosive devise, bigger than a firework but smaller than a small bomb.'

'So,' said a startled Eunice. 'A very small bomb.'

'Yes,' agreed Dougie. 'Like the one I reckon did for Tom Burleson in my kitchen.'

'Why, what's the daft devil think he was playing at?' asked Reenie plaintively.

'Oh, wake up!' snapped a testy Eunice. 'It was Dougie as was meant to perish – something must have gone wrong.'

Reenie put a hand up to her mouth and looked at Dougie. 'She's right,' he said. 'Tom was in explosives during the War, Anita told me. His knowledge of gas and way with a pilot light made him an ideal bomb setter. A dodgy business, apparently.'

Outside Mrs Robson was asking if Mr Peacock had put in an appearance, yet then Barry Hutchinson's voice advised her to look in the paper as 'daring Dougie's movements' were generally well covered there. 'I'll fill him in before I'm done,' Dougie said quietly. They sat in silence until the voices faded away. Eunice observed that Barry had played badly at York. 'Ah,' said Dougie. 'Now what was the story with that penalty?'

Reenie took up the theme, happy to be on more familiar ground. 'We were under pressure so he comes back to help in defense – course tackling's not his strong suit and he upends their lad in front of the ref. Clear penalty and they weren't going to miss. I thought Bob Guthrie was going to plant him one but Barry had scuttled up to the other end and stayed there out of the way.'

Dougie stared at the wardrobe. 'I blame myself. If I'd have been there he'd have stayed up field all game, I'd have made sure – I heard the kid got knocked about.'

'Oh, that was bad,' said Eunice. 'Their big lads at the back were kicking him for fun, he kept going though and laid one on for lover boy to miss near the end. He's gutsy, mind.'

'He'll need to be' said Dougie. 'Not be at this club for much longer with his ability.'

There was a further pause, someone in the far distance shouted 'twat!' then Reenie brought them back to more immediate matters. 'So, the long and short of it is that Tom Burleson tries to booby-trap your kitchen and puts himself in hospital instead.'

'That's about the size of it,' said Dougie.

'He's obviously lost his touch since Monte Casino,' said Eunice. 'Anyway Doug, what about our lot this Saturday, are we going to do it?'

'Hard to say – we're due a good show from Hutchy, if this lassie from the art school hasn't turned his head, like.'

'Is it serious then with them two?' asked Reenie.

'Well he took her to Newcastle for the day, so who knows?'

'And what about you and Anita?' asked Eunice.

Dougie paused then seemed to make up his mind to speak plainly. 'It's hit her hard; she's staying with her friend Mrs Dorman. I'm off up to see her later.'

'Will you be back for your tea?' asked Reenie.

'I'm not sure, don't bother doing me anything though. Here, let's get all this gubbins back in the box then I'll see to it.' He asked Eunice to fetch some brown paper and Sellotape from the office and to let Mrs Robson know he'd be in to see her as soon as the gasmen had finished at his house.

At the Northtown campus of Teesmade College of Art Harold was part of an earnest group of students studying a large print of a man falling backwards holding a rifle, having apparently been shot. Their teacher was taking them through a seminar on the power of images to touch lives, make as well as bear witness to history. They were learning that making pictures had lost its innocence, could no longer be a benign pursuit freighted with good intentions. Pointing a camera was a political act with consequences we could not predict. Photography was not to be viewed lightly. Yes indeed, thought Harold, just so. Grace put her hand up beside him. 'Yes?' said Colin keenly.

'You mentioned a French bloke who said that a negative was a ghost from the time between moments. What was he on about?'

'Jacques Chite? Well, I think we're back to the notion of photographs living in and out of time. Catching time, marking time, stretching it. Tempus fugitive. Somebody once asked a practitioner how long it had taken him to expose a particular image. He said 'thirty-two years and one hundred and twenty fifth of a second' – don't you think that's a marvelous answer?'

'Was this guy a semiologist then?' she asked.

'Probably,' said Colin.

Harold found something to say. 'Sometimes you have to wonder, don't you?'

The group looked in his direction. 'That's an interesting point Harold, will you develop it a bit?' asked Colin.

'Well it's all very well taking someone's picture without them knowing, but what happens if they see it and they don't like it?' Colin smiled at him in a way Harold didn't like and told him he had a wonderful way of going straight to the heart of the matter. Then it was time to go. Harold lingered and asked Colin again.

'It's partly to do with photography losing its innocence,' said Colin. 'There's a fascinating debate to be had around the politics of photography. The Family of Man people will argue that a photographer's integrity is reflected in his or her pictures, but once a print exists in the world whose is it, really? Think about the concept of copyright, think about the word – is it right to copy other people into a photograph? Is it acceptable only if we copy them right?'

'I don't know,' said Harold wishing he hadn't bothered.

'Is this prompted by your photo-essay in the paper, Harold?'

'Yes, I suppose it is. One of the pictures shows someone in a revealing light. It's caused a bit of a stir.'

'Did you know when you made the exposure Harold?'

'I don't really – I'm not sure.'

'Not your fault then and for all you know it might turn out for the best. This tells me that you're really engaging with your subjects, that's good and it's beginning to show in your pictures.'

Harold struggled with this as he cycled home. Dougie had been almost forgiving on the station last Sunday, perhaps he had done him a kind of favour after all. He wondered if Grace had seen his photo-essay and if she might need some help engaging with her subjects. Something to do with jumpers, as far as he could remember.

Dougie paused outside Mrs Dorman's front gate trying to remember what Bob Mullins had told him about tides and men who had affairs. Whatever it was he was in up to his neck and these were deep waters. Tom had been a proper clown and made a right mess of his kitchen and Anita. He hadn't been able to get much sense from her of late, but her friend seemed like a good sort, unlike Sarah Suggett who'd sung a rude song about his difficulties at the social and advised him 'to tie a knot in it at your age'. Others had been more understanding; Bob Mullins had let him know as long as the captain knew when to slip his cable a ship would always right itself. As long as off-the-field activity didn't disrupt the team it was all right with him. Dougie decided that when the waters were more settled he'd ask Reenie more about Mullins and his salty dog ways. Mrs Dorman let him in and cautioned that Anita was having a lie-down. He was parked in the front room and handed a copy of the *Daily Express,* which made him jump when he spotted a small feature on the back page headlined 'Northtown Crackers'. However, it was just another snooty and sloppily researched piece by a national deigning to cover one of 'the minnows' – weary emphasis was placed on "a sleepy but pleasant backwater" where "things have been stirring this season thanks to the canny stewardship of able seaman Bob Mullins and his seasoned second in command Douglas 'Dougie' Peacock, one of the lower league's most respected characters." It was forecast that "sparks would fly" on Saturday. He tossed it aside wondering how they thought sparks might fly in a backwater, especially now that Tom Burleson was out of harm's way. He walked across to the French windows and surveyed the garden. He'd learned that Horace Dorman ran a successful haulage firm and had fallen out with Burleson's over a delayed payment. He had never been there whenever Dougie had called and wasn't pottering about the borders now. It was all well-kept though and he spotted tomatoes ripening on poles in the greenhouse. As he took in the neat borders a scrawny black cat sauntered from the shrubs to glare back at him as it lifted its tail to spray the hydrangea.

'Ah, there you are,' said a tired voice behind him. Dougie held out an arm in welcome, but Anita just frowned and moved backwards out of the room without saying anything else. He felt a spasm of irritation then reminded himself that her husband was lying senseless in a hospital bed not far away. He guessed she'd gone to fill a kettle and found her in the kitchen. Mrs Dorman had made herself scarce.

Dougie tried hard. 'How is he Anita, have they been able to tell you much?'

'All they'll say is he's stable, but he took a bad head injury and it's too early to say. His broken leg will mend and they're doing some test on his chest. He's come out with some stuff mind; calls me Mrs Sausage, nobody would believe that French show and how many of the boys got through the lines. No mention of football, boilers or blasted Barry Hutchinson. The police tried to talk to him but all they got was some nonsense about munitions works in Gateshead. We're none of us any the wiser.'

'Have the police talked to you?'

'Oh yes. I told them all about us and what I think Tom was up to in your kitchen. It could have been you, you know.'

She filled up at this and he embraced her. 'Well at least it's all out in the open now, eh?'

'We should have done something sooner then it mightn't have come to this – and what's going to happen to Tom? It could be attempted murder.'

He held on to Anita and tried to gather his thoughts; the best outcome would be for Tom to rattle his clogs in hospital but that didn't sound likely. 'I'm just wondering if there's something I might be able to do about that.'

'How do you mean?'

'Well if I don't make a complaint to the police and cook up some cock and bull story then maybe there's a way out.'

She sniffed doubtfully and set about the tea things. 'Well if you can concoct a believable tale out of this little lot you're wasted at Northtown FC.'

He watched her graceful ankles as she moved about the kitchen and inwardly cursed the useless Herbert lying in state on emergency ward 10. Why couldn't he have made a proper job of it? 'It all depends on what they find at the scene of the accident.'

Anita's labile mood took a fractious turn and she shouted at him. 'Accident? Accident, you damn fool! What do you think he was doing in your kitchen while you were out? The game's up now, good and proper – what a lash up.'

'Yes but my boiler had been on the blink and he's been known to fix them personally, that lad with the camera said something. What if I was to let it be known that he might have mentioned something, you know in passing like. Just plant a seed.'

She said no more and they moved into the back room. 'Dougie, what sort of thing might they find at the scene of the – incident?' He explained about the contents of the wardrobe in the boot room but a lot would depend on what the boffins from Northern Gas found. 'Tom always was a secretive man. I put it down to his time in the War, it took a lot of them that way.' Dougie had spent his War training the troops at Caterick Camp and felt a brief respect for Tom the explosives ace with his battle-scared past. 'What did you do with all that stuff you found, then?'

'It's in Reenie Hardwick's airing cupboard.' He reached out and was permitted to hold her hand. 'This doesn't change anything between us. You know,' he said sternly.

Anita sipped her tea and watched the mechanism rotate at the bottom of Dulcie Dorman's ornamental clock on the mantelpiece. She wondered if they were heading for extra time.

CHAPTER NINE
BARRY UNBOUND

'Barry said he'd join us there for a quick one.'

'What, before the match tomorrow?'

'Yes,' said Shirley. 'Only the one then they're all off to spend the evening at Knotty Pines Country Club. Barry says he can hardly wait.'

Harold had put on his new shirt. 'What do you think?'

'Very nice.'

'Pea green, tab collar from Sir Henry's down Top Street – are you sure?'

'Harry you're the tops. Will Grace be joining us?'

'Yeah, she's coming along with Graham and his friend.'

'Graham and his friend, eh?' said Shirley as she pulled the front door to behind them.

'Yeah, Ally the boxer. Graham made friends with him when he was doing that set of studies down at Thumpers gym. They're not bad, you know.' Shirley didn't respond, so he asked her what was happening at Knotty Pines.

'I think it's just something to keep them out of trouble before the big match – the idea is to instil team spirit. And there's the Dougie Peacock question. Barry says nobody talks about it but they're all itching to know – do you know anything? The chairman's still in hospital, isn't he?'

'I believe so, lost his memory. I don't know any more – I'll be seeing Mr Peacock tomorrow, are you coming to the match?'

'Barry's giving me my ticket tonight.'

'And you're coming to the game tomorrow as well.' His cheek was rewarded with a dig in the ribs. He laughed and leaned into her as they passed.

'Don't Harry, last time we were down here there was a pile of dog muck big enough to need a night watchman.'

He reached out to help steady her and felt her weight against him as she held his shoulders. She was nearly as tall as he was and he could sense the form of her breasts. Grace had them too; he'd sneaked a look when they were working together in the library on the day he asked her out. He wondered what Barry would make of Grace and asked Shirley what he thought about the match. 'He's quite anxious about it but I've begun to see how chancy a footballer's life can be and how soon it can pass. He's had his opportunities in the big time, so helping Northtown win promotion could be his last bit of glory. He's expected to play well, so if the team loses he'll be one of the first to be moved on and he might not find another club. Even if they win he reckons they'll need a right clear-out for the higher league and he says Atkinson's certain to get sold, probably to Leeds.'

'What would Barry do if he had to stop playing?'

'Retrain to be a probation officer.'

'A what?'

'Don't say it like that, there's more to Barry than you'd think. He says a career in professional football is an ideal preparation – it's an odd world. You must have picked that up.'

'Well... I was shocked at how many of them smoke and I've seen fights break out, then there's this thing they do as they get changed before a match. Has Barry show... told you about it?'

'What do you mean, Harold?'

'Oh, I'll tell you later, I may have got it wrong anyway – I think I'm probably so focused on getting a good composition that I miss most of what's going on around me. I've noticed the players stop mucking about whenever Mr Mullins or Dougie are about.'

'Barry says you have to be frightened of the management otherwise the players take advantage. You're only as good as your last game.'

Harold thought about Alf Ramsey with his straight face and spaceman's voice, no wonder England had won. Then there was dour Don Revie: but he spoke fondly of his lads Little Billy and Big Jack, Sniffer and Gilesy. Rough love in a hard man's world as he soaped them down after the match. Perhaps Barry would make the best kind of do-gooder – not soppy but seasoned by experience. In a different life Alf Ramsey might have made a mental welfare officer. Life seemed full of possibilities, he was aware that Grace's mother worked in the Children's Department for Leeds Council.

Maybe she knew Little Billy?

'What are you laughing at, Harry?'

'Eh? Oh, something I was thinking about.'

'What?'

'Something I did manage to overhear down at the club. You know those two older women, one of them came down to Southend that time? Well, they seem to know anything that's worth knowing.'

'Go on.'

'Well, I heard one of them saying that Tommy Stanton reckoned he was good enough for the club to sell him to Juventos. The other one said they'd do better to sell him to Fray Bentos.'

Shirley smiled. 'They are funny. You really seem to be enjoying it, what's Grace doing for her project?'

'She's doing something at this big textile works in the town with lots of women workers.'

As they reached the Slaters Arms Reenie and Eunice tottered out with another woman resembling an old sparrow who'd spent too long in a puddle. 'Oh look you,' said Eunice as she smiled in Shirley's direction. 'We've just been saying to Barry he's to have an early night tonight.'

The third party glared at Harold and asked if this was the fellow who had come upon the lovers in London. 'Come on you,' said Reenie and rolled her eyes sympathetically in his direction.

'It's a disgrace, I say,' croaked Greta.

'Shut up,' said Reenie,. 'Time we got you home.'

They moved off away from the town in a swaying group driven forward fitfully by beer and belligerence. Harold watched them go thinking it might be nice to be an old woman, able to please yourself in a world apart from the dafter sex.

Inside the pub Barry was alone with a hardly sipped half of lager. Shirley sat down next to him and Harold asked about drinks. Barry waved him away with a frown, saying this would be his only drink 'for now'. Shirley asked Harold for a snowball so he went up to the bar where an old man took his time serving up a pint of Strong Arm and a snowball, the toothpicks arrangement with the glace cherry giving him some trouble. He seemed friendly enough and hadn't asked Harold his age so the customer lingered to chat. 'Are you able to get to the match tomorrow, then?'

'I can still get out and about nicely enough.'

'No, no – I meant with the licensing laws. Bound to be a big crowd.'

'I shouldn't think I'll bother,' he said and gave Harold an unmistakable will-there-be-anything-else smile.

As he went across to the other side of the room Harold caught something Barry was saying about 'They won't offer any of us anything yet in case we get turned over.' He hovered till Shirley met his eye, then he sat down by Barry. 'That landlord's slower than Bill Thompson isn't he? Now, Harry, you've got plenty of film for tomorrow, eh? And watch that linesman, this club's getting a reputation.' Harold grinned gamely and asked Barry if they would 'swing it'. 'God knows, anything can happen in this league, it's what makes it so much fun,' he said then stood up and left them.

'He's very tense,' said Shirley. 'They all are – if they don't go up most of the team will be shown the door and this business with the chairman is making people uncertain.'

'Oh don't start on that now, please Shirley.'

'Look, no one blames you, honestly. Most of the players find it hilarious – not Mr Burleson obviously, though that does have its funny side – they like to sing 'twas on the Friday morning when the gasman came to call' if Dougie's not around. It wasn't going to stay secret much longer. It might have been worse.'

'They say Mr Burleson has lost his memory.'

'Well there you are, then.'

Harold was about to ask Shirley what she meant, but his attention was diverted by the sight of Grace entering the pub with Graham and his tough-looking boxing chum. She came straight over to say hello. He thought she looked smashing with her hair all piled up and a flowery dress that came up over her knees. She lit up a Parkie and asked Harold for a lager and lime. Ally placed himself confidently beside Shirley and asked if that was Barry Hutchinson he'd passed on his way in. 'Oh yes,' said Harold. He's a friend of Shirleys.' And got up smartly to join Graham at the bar where a younger man was able to serve their orders quickly. 'So that's Ally, seems quite a character.'

'He's that all right,' said Graham with a grin.

Ally soon had the ladies laughing, Shirley being tickled to learn that Barry was known as 'Apollo' in local sporting circles. Graham laughed again and perched himself next to Grace. Harold looked more carefully at Ally and couldn't help wondering what this boss-eyed charmer was going to come out with next. He didn't have long to wait as Shirley pressed him for more details. 'Well if we recall that Apollo – for our purposes Barry – came from fabled Olympus – read London – but preferred the countryside, lots of farming land up here, so he moves to the north where he encounters a group of hardy shepherds gathered round an old man who was telling them remarkable things. That would be your Mr Peacock and the remarkable forecast would be Northtown's promotion, so, Apollo mucks in with them to help them in their perilous quest. 'He's not my Mr Peacock,' said Harold.

'No but you've managed to immortalise him,' said Shirley.

There was a pause for general laughter, which Harold found himself joining in, then Ally returned to his theme. 'As I remember there were some interesting goings-on involving a tortoise fitted with strings – a lyre, which Apollo manages to make a lovely sound with and probably some funny business with cloaks and daggers.'

'So how does that fit in with Barry's adventures in the north?' asked Shirley.

'Well, just that he is able to pluck magic from unlikely places and can help the shepherds to higher pastures, but we should bear in mind that mythology can only be interpreted, not understood.'

Harold couldn't help himself. 'You mentioned Mr Peacock. Well, it's common knowledge about – well, you know. Isn't there some fable of yesteryear foretelling his fate? Something that has an explosion in it somewhere with lovers blown off course and so forth?'

Ally thought about this. 'No,' he said. 'I think he's just been shagging the chairman's wife.'

More laughter, especially Harold noticed, from Grace. Their little group split off into two and he was able to ask her about her work with the women of West Auckland Woollens. They were able to chat comfortably about low light conditions and the decisive moment while the others debated sporting history and someone called Percy Phone. Shirley asked him how he knew so much Greek mythology so Harold and Grace began to listen. 'My father is a professor of Greek at Newcastle – there's a whole story with that which gets a bit Athenian – but despite the old get I got to like the stuff. '

Harold was on his third Strong Arm and felt bold enough to probe. 'How do you come to be here then, were the Greeks big on boxing?'

'Great fallings-out and separations, painful toil in barren spaces, hallucinations in the desert.'

'That sounds like Northtown,' said Graham.

'Yes, by way of Straynot Approved School, but now I am unbound and sit before you a chastened soul.'

Harold had never met anyone like this and sensed that even Shirley was bemused by it all. His admiration for Graham went up a good few notches though and his friend took centre stage for a while, telling them about the sporting club and finer points of boxing. Ally joined in and seemed to relax in Graham's company, explaining how boxing had helped him channel his anger to the point where he didn't need to assault his probation officer. Shirley was reading Harold's thoughts and shot him a glance so he worked his way forward with a few related tales from the dressing room before cuing in Grace for some weavers' talk. When she'd finished she rested an arm on his shoulder and passed him four shillings for more drinks.

'Well,' said Graham at ten o' clock. 'We're off now, look out for us in tomorrow's sea of faces.' Ally told Harold he wanted to see some of his pictures then they were off.

'What an interesting bloke,' said Harold.

'Yeah,' laughed Grace,

Shirley pulled out a number six and passed it over but Harold declined, as had both the other lads earlier when offered one. He looked around the room; most of the men had a cigarette on the go and several of the women too. Another woman was standing at the bar talking away with the bloke who'd served them before. The evening was becoming tousled and baggy, the people more inclined to look back at you if you weren't careful. He had been astounded recently by some photographs he'd seen at college. They'd been taken in London pubs, in one of them a woman was slapping someone and all the pictures looked hard and grainy. Being able to operate a camera was the least of it. He was beginning to see that a camera to a photographer was like a typewriter to a journalist and that sheer nerve was what you needed. And less 'sensitivity' than he sometimes felt right with. He asked Grace if she could take pictures in 'a place like this?'

'I'm not sure I'd want to.'

'Why not?' asked Shirley.

'Well, it would be a bit impertinent, people come here to drink and talk. I'm sure they wouldn't like it, certainly at first. If you're working closely with a subject then perhaps it's different. Then again – you remember that bloke in America they all go on about Harry?'

'Walker Evans?'

'Yeah him, apparently he didn't interact with his subjects much or even pretend to be interested in them but his pictures are brilliant, aren't they?'

'I really like those,' said Shirley.

'So maybe it's better to avoid pretending an interest or commitment you don't have, unless you really have one – if you see what I mean,' said Harold uncertainly.

'Do you want the Shunters to win tomorrow Harry?' asked Shirley.

'Yes I do actually; I'll be cheering for them.'

'Well, your pictures will reflect that and this will enhance their documentary worth,' said Grace in a voice designed to mock their tutors.

'Have you seen any of Graham's drawings from the boxing club?' he asked Shirley.

'No, he keeps that pretty much to himself. The last thing he showed me was that painting of the town clock after Duchamp. Pretty striking but no good if you wanted to tell the time.'

'When is last orders?' said Grace. 'Shall we all chip in and see what we can afford?' They found enough for three more halves and a bag of peanuts to share from the machine. This gave them enough energy to spend the next twenty minutes doing impressions of the staff at Teesmade. Grace showed herself a gifted mimic as she took off Hen Gunnars, a Swedish tutor from the school of painting in one of his elliptical chats with his friend, Boomie, 'Theese photofolk mek olmen of us all.'

'Is Boomie American?' asked Shirley.

'I think he flew in Bomber Command in the War,' said Grace.

Harold wanted to know about the offbeat reporter from the *Scene*, but Grace had never heard of him, or even read him. Soon it was kicking-out time and he found himself on the street in a lovely spring evening steering the ladies past a dispute, which had started in the pub and threatened to worsen at the bus stop. What amused Shirley was that the protagonists were at least seventy and the row seemed to be about onions. 'Allotments,' said Grace knowingly. 'My grandad has one, they inspire feelings of which men may not speak easily.'

'Where do you come from?' Shirley asked Grace.

'Wakefield.'

'No, I meant where do you live?'

'Not far. Do you mind walking back with me, then Harold can see you both home?'

'No, that's fine,' she said.

When it turned out that she lived very close to the pub he wondered why she'd asked for an escort. A chaste peck on the cheek and a warm 'see you next week' soon buoyed him up.

'She's nice,' said Shirley as they found their way back to Green Park.

'Yes. I've seen some of her pictures, she makes portraits with an old camera and large negatives.'

'Mmm, perhaps that makes the experience of being photographed feel different – a bit more intimate.'

They reached the town end of the park. Shirley motioned that she wanted to sit down on the first available park bench. They sat for a while then she asked him quietly what he thought of Graham's 'new friend'.

'I thought he was very interesting – very funny about life at the boxing club.'

'Yes, I loved that 'we'.'

'How d'you mean?'

'That 'we all call him Apollo' – I mean, I bet you can't move for classical scholars down on Bash Street.'

'Perhaps he picked it up with the boxing at his school.'

'You do know what kind of school he was talking about, don't you?'

Harold recognised her mocking tone and looked to the stars. 'It was a special kind of school – I should think he learned a lot of things there.'

'I expect he did,' she said and moved closer as she had in The National Gallery. 'Which one's the plough Harry?' He showed her how to get her bearings from some branches and use her fingers to trace the lights. She couldn't get it so he moved closer to hold her hand and move it about carefully. 'Do you think there's a football club out there or an art school somewhere?' she asked him.

'Bound to be, maybe Dougie Peacock's from Mars.'

'Come on Harry, let's get up the hill a bit.'

She linked arms with him and they sloped off companionably but, halfway up, she pulled him gently to a stop and kissed him properly on the lips. They drew apart but she smiled at him, so he moved forward for more. This one lasted quite a bit longer and developed into his most complex encounter yet. 'Come on,' she said when they'd finished. 'I'm sure we can find somewhere a bit more exclusive round here.'

He let her lead him down a discreet path that took them behind some bushes where a wall marked the limits of the park's eastern boundary. This showed him a side of the park, and of Shirley, he'd not seen before. He was about to tell her this when she sat down and patted the grass beside her. He could tell that Shirley was the kind of girl who followed the path with a heart and joined her. They spent the following forty minutes holding and snogging uninterruptedly. She also put her tongue in his ear twice which he found he liked and nibbled his lobe once, which he was less sure about. At one point her left breast made contact with his right forearm as their bodies became more attuned; he left it there and, when she didn't seem to mind, cushioned that part of her with his hand. This led to some more ear-nibbling so he changed his line of approach to some middle ground shoulder work. It all seemed to go very well and when they stopped for a break, Harold lay flat and she rested her head on his chest. He felt pleased with himself and a bit daft too. What did it all mean? Should he go further? Did Barry like to be nibbled – was it a lover's code? The longer they lay together behind the bushes the less it mattered.

CHAPTER TEN

INJURY TIME

Dougie rarely retired early and lying in an unfamiliar bed at Reenie's house hadn't helped him to relax. He made an effort to think about the game but it was futile; anything he and Bob Mullins might say would be beside the point. A draw would be no good so they'd just have to score more goals than the other lot, if the players hadn't got the message by now they never would. Making them sweat for their contracts was the best incentive, but this generation of footballers had it all soft, really; some of the knocks he and Mullins had taken would have poleaxed the likes of Barry Hutchinson, and that was just from the managers. This made him recall 'Mad Bill' McEwan his first gaffer when he'd been Barry's age – no nice five-a-sides then, just an Indian war dance before the kick-off. First chance you got elbow their goalie in the face then let their star man know you were around. It was kick or be kicked. Dougie knew though that some things had changed for the better, a young prospect such as Atkinson got some protection now and he basically despised throwbacks like Bill Thompson who would never play for this club again if he had any say in it. Mullins had only kept him on to help them get out of this division. He'd be hopeless higher up the league.

He lay and fretted about things which wouldn't normally bother him; would it be sunny or would rain be better, would Kenneth paint the penalty spot properly, would folk want pies in May? Anything to avoid thinking about Anita and Tom, Anita and him, Robert. He turned over for the umpteenth time, his neck ached, one side of his belly rumbled, he tried to find something of interest in Reenie's wallpaper but there was nothing doing, just daffodils and a recurring image of leaping rabbits. He got up and dressed then went back downstairs as quietly as he could. Reenie's front room was a shrine to her late brother Adolphous who'd been a merchant seaman. He perished one day in the storm tossed winter of '31 after putting out from Hartlepool in *The Leviathan*. Nearly the whole wall space was taken up with painting by numbers seascapes, a ship's wheel was propped in a corner and other bits of sailors junk could be found in the room. Dougie looked at a naive painting of a dog waiting forlornly on a quayside while the rest of the world went about its business. It was titled *The Hero's Return* but as far as he could see there was little in sight for the terrier to build its hopes on. He heard the stairs creak.

'You not able to sleep either?' said Reenie.

'No, I'll be better sitting up.'

'Have I to put the kettle on?'

'Aye, you can do.'

After half an hour's aimless nattering over the tea Reenie drew a deep breath to ask Dougie what he wanted to do about 'this business with you know who'.

'Well,' he said. 'It's out of my hands really.'

'But you've been up to Mrs Whydoyoumaflips, what was she like?'

'In a bad way, blames herself for that business Tom pulled. Anyway, I tell her it's my fault and should never have put her in

172

the position to begin with, so then she sets on wailing that don't I love her anymore. I can't say owt but it ends in more tears. It's a bad lookout whichever way you look at it.'

'What's that path you've to follow in times of doubt?'

'Don't start that, Reen.'

'No listen Doug, it's like when our Dolly got carried off. Our mam said then that there were tides in the affairs of men and that sometimes you got wet feet.'

He paused out of respect and gave the impression of being moved. 'You mean that once something's done it's done?'

'Exactly and you can't break eggs without making an ill wind or blowing somebody up.'

'Yes, I see what you mean,' he cut in. 'But if she and I hadn't clicked like we did Tom would still be happy rolling out boilers, Anita would probably be sipping sherry with the Ladies Magic Circle...'

'And you'd be?'

This time he really was moved and disclosed for the first time to a third party the depth of feeling he had for Anita and acknowledged that, when the tide of love rolled in, you could do no more than take the path with the wind, and blow the consequences.

'Exactly,' said Reenie. 'If she'd been happy with Tom she wouldn't have strayed, she's not the type. She must think a lot of you Dougie and now you and your Robert have made up, what's to stop you?'

He sighed and nodded. 'It's true enough. He's coming home soon, been asking after you as well.'

'So what's stopping you and Anita?'

'What do you think people will say, she's well known in this town – still it's all out by now, isn't it?'

173

'Exactly. Most people will understand and if the team wins tomorrow, they'll say it was all for the best.'

'Come again?'

'Well they might think that the chairman's wife put the spring back in your step and this pepped up the team. You've both come back to life.'

'So, what you're saying in effect, like, is that the prospects for me and Anita come down to Barry Hutchinson after all?'

Over at Knotty Pines Country Club Dave Stanton opened a window to let the bad air out. The first signs of daylight were showing around the golf course as birds stirred themselves for the dawn chorus. 'Fuckin' 'ell man,' said someone. 'You got a dead rat up your arse, Hutch?'

Harold's arrangements for match day were to meet up with Ernie Todd by the club office at one thirty to receive their special match day passes, then be escorted to their allotted places behind one of the goals. He'd spent most of Saturday morning cleaning his camera, packing and re-packing his press man's bag, rolling off film and looking at a handbook on action photography. Once he felt prepared he made a pot of tea and settled himself with the previous day's *Northern Scene*. Graham hadn't come home and Shirley was still in bed but things were happening fast for Harold. Thanks to Shirley he'd sampled drugs and increased his sexual experience to the power of ten, at least. The memory of their tryst in the park was still fresh: unlike his drug taking he could tell what all the fuss with sex was about and was keen to have a go with Grace, or Shirley again if the fancy took her. He felt especially good that she'd chosen him, that he was as good as Barry Hutchinson in her eyes, at snogging anyway.

Barry was the subject of some coverage in the paper; he was Northfield's 'key man', a flair player from the higher divisions capable of turning a game "with an insouciant drop of those wily shoulders" or "playing in his fellows with a deft, defense-splitting pass". A warning note was sounded about Tranmere's "combative back line" pointing out that Barry and "young Atkinson" should expect no quarter to be given. Bill Thompson's absence was also felt to be a problem. There was a brief mention of Mr Burleson and the goodwill felt for this "unassuming Vulcan of local industry". Then a note that Coach Peacock "would be back at his post following a family illness, now resolved". It also referred to how deeply Dougie cared about "his beloved Northtown" as his "occasional rushes of blood to the head" showed. He took Shirley a cup of tea up and was asked to leave it outside her door and look out for her after the match.

Post match debate, York City Social Club, January 1983.

CHAPTER ELEVEN

TOWN STIRRED BUT NOT SHAKEN

Match report from the *Northern Scene* 6 May 1968:

Northtown Athletic 2 Tranmere Rovers 1

Just as there are no second acts in American lives so there are no second chances in football. The last instalment of the Shunters' switchback ride to division three proved to be in keeping with all that had gone before in this remarkable season-long journey. Their loyal fans have certainly had a ticket to ride and today was no exception as their beloved lads missed points, got stuck facing the wrong way, ran out of steam, over-stoked the engine but finally, gloriously, chuffed asthmatically towards the light at the end of the tunnel to emerge blinking in the light of promotion as Tranmere conked out behind them. The visitors from Beatleville played their full part in an enthralling contest which hung still uncertain until the final moments when a referring decision, which will live long in the memories of all who saw it, tipped the balance in Northtown's direction.

The denouement could not have been foretold as Tranmere kicked off on a perfect spring Saturday and immediately put the home goal under pressure. Patterdale on the left caused difficulties with his close control and accurate passes and

Burton in the home goal had to be off his line smartly to deal with a teasing cross as Morrisey went up to challenge him for a header. Both men ended up in the netting and Coach Peacock was required to attend Burton before play could continue. Skipper Sproates discussed the incident at length with the Tranmere man and soon engaged him in a meaty challenge once the game got underway again. In fact tackles were soon flying in from all quarters, Hutchinson in particular coming in for rough treatment as the men from Merseyside 'got among' the home forwards. The first real opportunity fell to Atkinson when he ran bravely at the Tranmere defense, beat his man and shot just over. This seemed to inspire his fellows and the Shunters enjoyed a spell of dominance without really troubling the Tranmere goal. Just as it seemed certain that Northtown would breakthrough disaster struck. Atkinson again made good progress along the wing but was blatantly checked by Woodhead the tough full back who left the gallant youth clutching his ankle. The linesman signaled a foul but the referee, Mr Pollard from Peterborough, waved play on. This was a puzzling, not to say unpopular decision with the large crowd but worse was to follow. Woodhead, looking suitably lumpen and delinquent with his 'skin head' hairstyle hoofed the ball upfield where Dawson struggled to control it first time. Patterdale was onto it in a flash and exchanged passes with Pinter before racing goalwards to place it expertly beyond a badly exposed Burton. One nil to Tranmere and the signal for their travelling supporters to find their tongues and get behind their favourites. They also sang a ribald song involving the linesman, Coach Peacock and the chairman's wife, but order was soon restored when Northtown equalised. This goal also had an element of controversy and involved Woodhead again; a home throw-in appeared to come to nothing as the Tranmere man gained possession, but for reasons best known to himself he passed behind him, without looking, to Hutchinson, who was full of running and seemed to be everywhere. The Northtown dynamo took off at speed to lay the ball to Stanton who blasted home and raised the rafters. In the general mayhem Woodhead and Hutchinson were seen to exchange blows but the referee took a lenient view and simply admonished the pair. Woodhead wished to discuss the incident further with the official but gained nothing but a booking for his troubles and much mockery from the crowd, who were greatly enjoying the proceedings.

Half-time arrived soon after this and Coach Peacock, Northtown's man for all seasons, dashed onto the field of play to escort Hutchinson lest further difficulties ensued. Talk in the press box told of dark doings and explained Woodhead's woe; it seems that the equalizer resulted from some craft on Hutchinson's part as he called "roll it back wack" in a Merseyside accent, then took full advantage of the misunderstanding. It was generally agreed that Woodhead only had himself to blame having put one over on Atkinson and being stupid to boot. So, it was all square and all to play for.

The second half was a tense affair as Tranmere dug in to allow little latitude for Northfield to break the deadlock and the visitors' lamentable lack of ambition meant that much home possession came to naught. The visitors' most enterprising men, Patterdale and Morrisey, by now limping noticeably following another stern challenge from Sproates, were virtual passengers and mounting frustration was the theme. The nearest either side came to a goal was a long-range effort from Tilley of Tranmere, which Burton saved well, and a twenty-yard power blaster from Fidler that rattled Tranmere's crossbar and roused the home supporters. Despite their marvelous encouragement

Northtown's fans were tantalised as shots were absorbed by Tranmere's guardians. The second half was held-up while Morrissey was brought round and declared fit to re-enter the field of combat meant that injury time would be allowed but the town clock was running down when Tommy Rott gained possession over to the far right of Tranmere's goal. The wily Pole looked up and lofted over a high cross, nearly every outfield man was in or about the penalty box as the ball described a leisurely arc. At least six men went up for the ball but the outstretched hands of Bob Rollocks, Tranmere's bouncing bomb of a goalkeeper, took the ball and the clutch of players fell in a great heap. Rollocks rose first and made to throw the ball out to Patterdale when the crowd erupted into raucous laughter; the Tranmere goalie stood holding the ball with his shorts about his knees and nothing beneath them. The referee blew his whistle shrilly and, once more, Hutchinson appeared to be at the centre of things as an enraged Rollocks dealt him a blow, which sent him back to the ground. This gave the cue for fully five minutes of conflict of one sort or another as players aired their views and many an arm was raised in disputation. Eventually a fleeting peace was restored and it became clear that the disgraced goalie and the confused striker had both been sent off. And Northfield had been awarded a penalty which the referee, who must be accorded a note of commendation for his calm and reasoned approach to a potential powder keg of a football match, made it clear that enough time would be allowed for the kick to be taken. High drama at the last and Skipper Sproates stepped forward to take responsibility. With the minimum of preparation he ran up at a nod from the referee and hammered the ball past the luckless Woodhead, who had gone in goal and was now called upon to pick the ball out of the net as the stadium erupted. More time was allowed for Tranmere to take a brief kick off then full-time was signaled. Northtown had done it after the most remarkable match of a remarkable season and the crowd made ready to salute the conquering heroes.

Having moved into the goal area after a rattled-looking ref had blown for time Harold and Ernie could do nothing but push their way into the throng and let it take them with it. He'd seen the famous pictures of the 1923 'White Horse' final and reckoned that a crowd of 15,000 at Northfield was about the same in terms of weight, mass and inconvenience. The only Bobby he could see was trying to retrieve his helmet from two old men who were tossing it playfully across the heads of a static group. He didn't seem that bothered and one of the old guys returned the helmet when the other shouted 'here they are now'. Harold could see some activity up in the director's box as men in suits stood to make way for a tired set of players. They shuffled in grinning and waving to the cheering throng below. He thought he could see Shirley among them with an older woman but they'd gone when he was able to look again. He could see most of the team though; Burton the goalie grinning like a lad, Fidler with his sharp face and Ted's quif making Stanton laugh about something, Sproates with his arm around Atkinson who looked bewildered, then Rott the strange Polish winger who'd laid on the penalty but looked keener on getting back to his digs at Durham and Guthrie, whose likeable personality seemed to be his biggest asset to the team, passing round cups of tea. Finally and to the biggest cheer so far came Mullins the manager beaming tolerantly and milking the moment before Guthrie signaled for quiet. Harold heard a voice behind him say 'twas' on the good ship Northtown' and the manager spoke to his public. His gruff voice carried well but

181

Harold found the content odd; salted with sailors' talk and 'uncharted waters before us' the whole thing had a valedictory air as if he and the rest of the grandstand were saying farewell from the stern of an old ship which was soon to pull away from the crowd on the dock below, leaving a great empty space.

That feeling of loss and things changing came home to him more forcibly when he failed to pick out Barry or Mr Peacock. It was all over now and what was going to happen next? Ernie Todd appeared and asked where the 'man of the moment' was?

'Barry Hutchinson?' said Harold.

'Aye,' said the genial cameraman. 'The canny cockney, I shouldn't think football like that's been seen in a northern town since Dougie Peacock's day. Remarkable really.'

'I can't spot him either.'

Ernie smiled and said, 'Well that's another story. I predict some interesting developments at this club by the time those uncharted waters are tackled, might be more than a fresh lick o' paint and a trim of the sails.'

'Why does Mr Mullins talk like Captain Pugwash, Ernie?'

'Before he went into football management Bosun Mullins captained a ship and saw action in the War – a very interesting man, crackers like but then he'd have to be to manage this lot.'

'Hang on,' said Harold. 'Here's Hutch now... look.'

The players had begun to clap and laugh good-naturedly as they made space for a bemused-looking Barry who smiled vacantly and waved hesitantly in the general direction of the crowd. Then he fell backwards into Dawson's arms and seemed inclined to stay there, so a chair was found for him while a beaming Bosun Mullins crouched to share a few words with him. There was still no sign of Dougie and Harold began to wonder.

The crowd had begun to thin out and Ernie produced his press camera. 'Come on,' he said to Harold. 'This is history in the making.'

He followed Ernie's example and spent the next half hour catching his impressions of the happy mass; then, once he was able to get closer, of the players and manager who were happy to stay put like Russian generals before a different kind of May Day parade. This thought returned him to Shirley; since taking up with Barry she'd seemed to have lost some of her interest in Vietnam or what was cracking off behind the Iron Curtain. He'd kept his usual weather eye on things and been genuinely upset by the Luther King killing but, beyond the usual reflections that he was glad to be who he was where he was, he was no nearer feeling interested by or involved with politics. He'd heard talk at college of young photographers in some of the difficult parts of the world risking their lives to bear witness to what was wrong, the clear implication was that notions of aesthetics or 'composition' were luxuries in such 'contexts'. He could appreciate how brave and necessary all this was but it didn't sound like much fun – no doubt he'd feel different if he lived in Prague. No events were unhistoric for the people caught up in them, and if love had pushed politics out of the window for Shirley, who was to say what was more important?

He got some nice shots of Mr Mullins chuckling with his crew, then wandered off towards a space by the players' tunnel. In the little dugout, where so much emotion was expressed during a game, he found Dougie sitting quietly by himself. 'Hello son,' he said when their eyes met. Harold moved forward and sat down beside him. The older man acknowledged his presence by moving over a little to allow him space, but didn't say anything, simply looking out with a hand on each knee and breathing steadily. Harold did something very similar and found himself pulled gradually into a detached and restful state. Everybody seemed happy in the moment and in no hurry to move away from it. Harold could see lots of figures standing to talk or moving slowly through the light but the main experience for him was the lulling sound of murmured conversation around the dugout and amiable bumps or scrapes of movement behind and above him. He was free in his own skin and hoped that Dougie felt that way too, he sat back and shut his eyes. He didn't lose touch completely but felt suspended in something like a warm sea where aqueous sounds and sirens voices floated about him. At one point Mr Mullins was waving a port-side farewell to Barry and Shirley as they were borne away on a jewel-encrusted clipper crewed by the players. Dougie was in there somewhere calling on the men to 'look lively'. Then he woke up and Dougie told him that there were some pictures to be had 'back stage like.'

Harold tumbled out into the bright sunshine and followed Dougie to the dressing rooms. There were quite a few people milling around in the corridor and he overheard Eunice's voice saying that Barry's next game would be at the Newcastle City Hall. When they reached the inner sanctum he was surprised to find Shirley there with her sketchbook and a bottle of beer. Most of the people in the packed little room seemed to have one and he was soon handed his own 'Strongarm' in a short amber bottle. He set to work getting a few shots of Shirley; taking care to include Barry stretched out behind her on a bench looking very much the worse for wear. Just about everyone he'd come into contact with at the club drifted in and out at some point over the next ninety minutes so, he was able to document the whole thing from a rickety vantage point on some stacked chairs in the corner. The beer ran out eventually so the crowd dispersed to the Slaters Arms with a skittish Eunice in charge, leaving Barry, still prone and puzzled, Shirley, Dougie, Tommy Rott and Harold. He could hear Sproates and some of the others chortling in the corridor with Bill Thompson, who'd brought the ale in wooden crates and tapped his bent nose knowingly when Mr Mullins asked about it. Harold was tired of trying to arrange the music of time through his camera and put it to one side. He immediately saw a potential picture he would never get but thought *sod it* and took a swig of his beer instead.

'Not bad yeah, Doug?' said a happy Tommy.

'Aye,' said Dougie. 'You in town tonight?'

'Aye Doug, got to stay with Big Bill.'

'Well,' said Dougie. 'Northtown beware.'

Harold went to talk to Shirley. 'What's the matter with Barry, is he all right?'

'It's all been a bit much for him,' she said.

Harold had noticed that Shirley Foxton seemed to have that effect on you, but kept this to himself. 'Their goalie gave him a right thump, didn't he? It wasn't Barry's fault what happened was it?'

'Well,' she said quietly. 'We'll never know, but Barry's bravery won the match, I'd say.'

'Yes, I suppose it did, and he did ever so well for the first goal as well, didn't he?'

Barry began to stir and slowly got himself up into a sitting position, beckoning to Shirley for her bottle of beer. He fortified himself with a long draught, burped expansively and fixed his gaze on the coat hooks across the room. 'It's all a bit of a blur after I went up for that high ball, there seemed to be so many of us – I remember holding on to someone as we came down then the next thing was Dougie helping me off the field. Did their keeper deck me or something?'

'That's right,' said Dougie. 'On account of how you yanked his shorts down — ref sent the pair of you off and give us the penalty.'

'And Skip put it away,' said Barry wonderingly.

'And we won promotion,' said Shirley.

'And you were man of the match,' said an incredulous Dougie. 'I've never seen you run around like that before. I'd say Bob Rollocks did you a favour, you'd still be running around like a man possessed if he hadn't knocked your block like he did.'

Barry assured Dougie he'd never run like that again and Shirley gave Harold a look, which he acknowledged, by looking at the floor and Dougie left them to it. He helped Shirley do some tidying up while Barry took a shower. His shin pads had fallen down behind a bench; Harold picked one up and put it in his camera bag.

CHAPTER TWELVE
IN THE PICTURE

'How did he take it?'

'Didn't react at first, but I'm used to that. Then he looked out of the window and said "Beats me how they do it". Could have meant anything.'

Dougie sipped Mrs Dorman's nice tea and munched her shortbread while Anita looked through the French windows. He was finding the whole thing a chore. This was a series of problems he couldn't shout at or apply the unbreachable silence of men to until they went away. He knew that Anita wished him to take a leading hand in their troubles and could see the sense of this, but Coach Peacock was well out of his depth, and he could see rocks ahead. Reenie would have had a surer grasp of the situation, but asking for her advice was out of the question. He shoved another biscuit into his mouth and tried to make it last. Eventually he said, 'Well you know him best, how did he seem to you?'

'He gave me a couple of choruses of *Barnacle Bill the Sailor* then he closed his eyes,' she said and began to weep again. This time she let him comfort her and it gave him some confidence. 'Well that's one of the names folk have for Mullins, not that Tom would ever call him that, always had a proper respect for his manager, even when he was wigging him over that unfortunate trip to Stockport and .. well, you know. Anyway, shows something went in.'

'Oh, do you think so Dougie? He'd have been so proud, he always looked forward to be chairman of a third division football club, meet new men in their boardrooms, rub shoulders with the likes of Queen's Park Rangers.'

'Aye well, they got promoted as well so we'll not be rubbing-'

'Yes, but Tom's not to know that you fool – oh, listen man he's a cracked pot and they don't know if they can fix him.' She pulled away from him in anger and went off to another part of the house. Which was another thing to sort out soon. Horace Dorman had lingered the last time Dougie had called to have some some bluff chat about this and that, which he'd steered towards the explosion and how long it might take to reassemble Dougie's kitchen. They'd parted with an understanding that the matter would soon be cleared up. This had been last week. He sat down and poured another cup of tea, putting the whole mess out of mind by reliving the afternoon's events, marveling at the extraordinary display Hutchinson had conjured up. Of all the young men he'd bawled, bollocked or cosseted into passable athletes Barry Hutchinson was the only one he could say he didn't understand, couldn't fathom. Or as Reenie had put it 'there's more in his head than lice'. Perhaps it was that young lass from college he'd taken up with. As he well knew a lady in your life tended to make things interesting and there was no denying the lass had a nice way with her, like Robert's girlfriend. This lifted his spirits and he decided that as things were well again there then most things were mendable. He got up and went to find Anita.

'Look Barry, you've got to get your head tested, down at the hospital. You don't look right.'

He was sitting vacantly in the living room trying to make some sense of a large, striking portrait by Graham of one of his boxing pals. The subject was placed naked in a pugilistic pose against a neutral background and the artist had seen fit to frame the thing with old co-op tea packets stuck down on the canvas. Anyone would have found the image diverting but something in Barry's manner conveyed deep feeling. 'Shirl,' he said piteously. 'It's not just the knock from their keeper. I was up late last night then I swallowed one of those pills to calm me down a bit. Only it wasn't one of them I showed you, it was one of Thommo's blast-off jobs. I'm only just coming down now. I feel lousy – can I have a drink?'

'Are you going to come to the hospital with me then?'

Barry thought about this. 'Where's Harry?'

'Upstairs having a lie down after all the excitement.'

'He's got the right idea.'

'I'm not letting you go to sleep until a doctor's seen you.'

'Well how are we supposed to get there? I don't even know where it is.'

'Ambrose next door has just got a banger. If I ask him he'll take us.'

'That's not Ambrose Fogarty is it?'

'Who? No, I don't know but I think he's a footer fan – just sit quietly while I slip round to see if he's in.'

Dougie found Anita smoking in the back garden. He considered it a filthy habit in general but it did, in a woman, stir his desire and there was no getting round the fact that Anita Burleson was a very classy smoker. He walked over to Dulcie Dorman's birdbath and sat down on the bench behind it. Anita made another slow circuit of the flowerbeds then joined him. 'He keeps it very well Nita.'

'It's her that does the garden.'

'She's a resourceful woman, she's looked after you well enough.'

'Oh, Dougie do you think I haven't thought about that? I know I've got to go home but I just can't face that place, not on my own.'

He let this lie briefly, then said, 'But you don't need to be on your own, Nita.'

'Dougie man, talk sense. I cannot take home a new fella five minutes after Tom's blown himself up.'

'Why not? Nita I love you – now more than ever.'

He thought she might take off like an affronted pigeon to another part of the garden. A small part of him wanted her to but the greater part could see that this was one tide he'd have to take his socks off to. She didn't move and sought out his hands to place hers, prayer-like inside his stubbly sportsman's mitts. 'None of this has changed anything for me either,' she said. 'I can't see how we're to manage it though, can you?'

Dougie was feeling firm and ready for anything again. His Kings Cross capacities came back. Sproates must have felt something similar when he put away that penalty, there was only going to be one outcome. 'We're off down to that hospital to tell him,' he said.

Ambrose knew the way to Northtown Memorial Hospital having visited or been visited there a number of times in his biker days. He explained this to Barry on the way over as the banger, a whiffy old Singer with sunburnt upholstery that was making the poorly passenger queasy, had been a part exchange deal including his old BSA 350. Further intelligence from the

190

driver about the five-bike pile-up which had curtailed his rockin' days and set his old mum's nerves jangling made Shirley change the subject. 'Did you go to the game this afternoon Ambrose?'

'Oh yeah, what a laugh. You did their keeper eh? Canny or what?'

'I didn't do anything to the great ape – I can't remember anything about it anyway.'

'He did though didn't he?' scoffed Ambrose.

'Yes,' said Barry peevishly and fell into a sort of trance for the rest of the journey while Shirley asked after Ambrose's mum and life at the local blacking factory.

The Memorial Hospital was a tall redbrick infirmary built with care at a time when there had been money and imagination to spare. It was like a church too because anyone going into the place became serious. The stern salving scent, purposeful bustle and unfussy utility told you it was not somewhere you went lightly and might not leave. Ambrose's gormless prattling about crashes had left Barry edgy and anxious so that when a nurse in a crushed wimple approached she was able to identify him as the patient. Shirley explained the position to her as Ambrose loitered in reception. She accompanied Barry down to a side room where the nurse assured them that a doctor would see them soon. He reclined effortfully on a dull plum examination couch and told Shirley his head was hurting. She sat beside him and held his hand.

It wasn't long before a doctor came; an African of the darkest hue Shirley had ever seen called Dr Mbargo. Barry took him in his stride and complied with requests to watch fingers, open wide as a piercing light was shone in his eyes, and tell him of any stiffness, pain or odd sensations. As soon as the

191

examination was over Dr Mbargo asked Barry what had really happened when everyone had gone up for that high ball. 'Most remarkable, we were standing directly behind the goal but nobody could say with any certainty how things came to pass.'

'Yeah,' said Barry. 'That just about sums it up really.'

'Most remarkable, though their goalkeeper was not justified in the actions he took, thereby presenting you before me as a concussed but unbroken sportsman of the highest rank.'

'Yes,' said Barry wearily.

'So he's all right then?' asked Shirley.

The Doctor stood up straight. 'He will be fine but must spend the next twenty-four hours peacefully with an uninterrupted sleep. I will prescribe something to aid the process.' He wrote out a script and gave directions to the pharmacy. 'But first you must rest. Stay here and I will see you in twenty minutes.'

When the Doctor had left Barry said, 'I wish he'd make his mind up, I thought he said I'd be all right?'

'He did Barry, they're being careful that's all. There's no rush.'

'And I'm not taking any more pills, I'm finished with that game – I'm fed up with soccer too, everyone thinks it's a lark but it isn't.'

'Barry, you've had a bang on the head, also that stuff of Thommo's is wearing off. You're bound to feel this way for a bit. It'll pass, poor Harold was like a bear with a sore head after that time at Southend.' Barry said nothing but lay back and let Shirley hold his hand again. After what had seemed like a long time but was only ten minutes when she checked, Shirley heard voices somewhere outside the room. Voices she recognised. 'Barry listen, isn't that Mr Peacock out there?'

Barry bent his aching head. 'Yes it is. Listen Shirl, nip out and see what's going on.'

She poked her head round the door and saw Dougie with Anita Burleson coming towards her. She caught the tail end of him saying 'no knowing how he'll take it' then he saw her. She said 'It's Barry' in a whisper and beckoned them into the side room. Anita hesitated till Dougie motioned for her to come too then they came in to see the man of the match. Dougie moved to the end of the bench to give him a look hovering somewhere between sympathy and annoyance. Anita hung back looking very tense.

'It won't matter if we just see how the lad is,' he said to her. She nodded and came forward to look at Barry.

'Shirley insisted I came here,' he said.

'Good job an' all, too much excitement in one day, eh?' said Dougie to Shirley.

Barry sat up and swung his legs over the bench. 'What brings you here anyway, is someone else hurt?'

'We've come to visit Tom,' said Anita.

'How is he?' asked Shirley. 'I read in the paper about the explosion, it sounds pretty bad.'

'He's very poorly,' said Anita. 'They say his short-term memory has been badly affected but there's something gone wrong with his... well, everything really. One of the doctors I spoke to said it was some sort of aphasic trauma something or other. He reckoned it might have been coming anyway and that the explosion brought it forward and made it worse. I don't think they know to be honest, they're moving him to a special place at Newcastle next week. More tests and whatnot.'

Barry stood up. 'I'm really sorry Mrs Burleson, he always seemed like a good chap to me, I'm sure we all put on a special effort for him today.'

She burst into tears so he went over to embrace her. This proved too much for Dougie so he went back out into the corridor. Shirley followed and found him staring blankly at the porridge-coloured wall. 'It's a rum do this is lass,' he muttered. 'Don't you and Barry get caught up in a game like this.' They became aware of Dr Mbargo hovering and they all went back to Barry's side room where he was still cuddling Mrs Burleson.

'I see you are greatly improved Mr Barry,' boomed the jovial medic. 'But I must look into your eyes too before you can go.'

Dougie muttered something to himself as the Doctor pulled out his headset and torch to submit his patient to further scrutiny. After more careful work and assessment Barry was declared fit for discharge with a note to Shirley about 'quiet nights and restful days to come'.

'So that's that then,' said Dougie sourly. 'Go home and put your feet up, all right for some folk.'

Doctor Mbargo turned to Dougie. 'Oh yes, our bold Olympian may regain the wings of a dove given rest and appropriate recreation. And who are you?'

'Eh? Oh, I'm from the club too, but we're here to see someone else. We looked in on Hut... Barry once we knew he was in.'

'Yes I see, and who is your main concern?'

'We've come to visit my husband,' said Anita. 'He's on Wilson Ward.

'Ah yes, a most interesting case.'

Dougie had been badly rattled by the way things seemed to be going, particularly the reference to 'my husband' and being challenged by the consultant. 'Well if it's that interesting can you tell us what's wrong with him?'

'You should discuss this with Mr Fall his specialist – a most accomplished man. I belong to the junior ranks only and must leave you now.'

Dougie glowered at the door as it closed behind Dr Mbargo and Anita put an emollient hand on his arm. 'Listen pet, I think we should all go up to see Tom now.'

'What on Earth for? I thought we were going to tell–'

'Not now Doug, I can't, not like this. Seeing Barry might help Tom and it's no good coming if we can't try to make him feel a bit better, is it?'

Dougie looked in disbelief at Barry and shook his head. 'Why not? Let's have a party, the way things are going I may as well send out for Sarah Suggett and the town band.'

'Look,' said Barry. 'Maybe now isn't really the best time...'

Anita turned to Shirley and said, 'Please come, it can't do any harm and poor Tom's in a dreadful way. You could talk him through the match Barry, he'd love to hear about it all.'

Barry smiled at Dougie. 'What I can remember of it.'

The women led off along the corridor while Dougie blathered away in Barry's ear – 'three sheets to the wind' – don't say anything unless he speaks first' – liable to come out with God knows what class of nonsense' – 'she doesn't help acting like a blessed water pump' – 'if you take my advice son'. Barry was glad when they got to the lift and Dougie shut up as they crowded into the metal cage. Wilson was a small dormitory ward with side rooms at one end. Tom was in the furthest one and sidling past the occupied beds had been a sobering experience, so by the time the nice nurse had left them with Tom they were quite subdued. Especially Shirley; up to this point the accounts she'd had from Barry and others had given a slightly comic aspect to the affair. She knew that Mr Burleson had been burnt but felt he'd get better. Now that she saw him bandaged and shell-shocked she thought him more likely to die. He seemed aware that there were people in the room but not who they might be. She expected Anita to be first to speak but Barry surprised her by saying hello to Mr Burleson and asking him how he was.

He was rewarded with a watery smile and a hand movement, which seemed to beckon him closer. Barry sat by the bed to give Tom a colourful and lengthy account of the 'marvelous show' against Tranmere, how Mr Mullins had geed them up to do their best for their chairman and how proud they'd felt once it was all over because Northtown was such a grand club. He left out the more picaresque elements and didn't bother to tell him about his own reasons for attending the hospital. When he'd finished Tom smiled again and asked Barry 'to tell the men the tide has turned in our favour'.

Anita was noticeably moved by Barry's narrative and even Dougie gave him a tepid smile. 'Thank you so much Barry,' she said. 'I think we'll take it from here.'

Shirley waited till they were alone in the lift to embrace him and tell him how kind he'd been. 'Poor devil,' he said. I might have been telling him anything.'

'Something seemed to go in, you could tell.'

'Perhaps. He's going to need some looking after though.'

'Anita was telling me that Dougie wants them to tell Tom they're together now, but she's not so sure about it.'

'Well you can't see him taking much in any way. They'd be better off waiting to see how it goes – Dougie can be a bit dense sometimes.'

Ambrose had left a message in reception that he'd promised to run his mother over to his Uncle Pete's but would get back as soon as he could. They sat down in the wood-paneled vestibule. 'He's really bad, isn't he?' said Shirley.

'Yeah,' said Barry. 'A trip to Newcastle might only tell them what they already know.'

'Poor Anita.'

'Can you understand me Tom?' she asked. 'It's me Anita, Dougie's come to see you as well. The team's won promotion.' Mr Burleson just looked back at her from somewhere beyond reach, then he picked a bit at his blanket looked at Dougie, then closed his eyes. Anita burst into tears but this didn't get to him, either. Dougie stood close to her and she allowed him to take her arm.

'Come on pet, I might as well be the man on the moon for all he knows.'

'He can still hear us, you know.'

'Have I to leave you with him for a bit?'

She gave him a fleeting smile and slight nod so he passed back through the ward into another corridor where he found a chair and a picture on the wall to look at; roses in a vase in an empty room. It was the kind of painting he liked – the roses looked like roses and he'd been in a room like the one in the picture at Mrs Dorman's house, the whole thing was well done, sensible, it reminded him of his own life. He wondered if they taught them how to turn out pictures like that up at the Art college. As hospitals went this one wasn't too bad. They'd smartened it up a bit since his wife's accident and the one he'd been to at Bolton could have done with a few nice pictures to stop you thinking too much. It wasn't working though and it wasn't long before his anger with Tom Burleson bubbled up again. The bloody fool had tried to put him in here, now he was lying up there like a booby making life ten times harder than it needed to be. Dougie's doom was lightened by the coloured doctor who came into view and stopped to pass the time of day. 'We must cheer you up, Mr Dug. In our hospitals the patients naturally come first but they also serve who only sit and wait, as your Mr Milton might observe.'

Dougie was properly shaken now. He liked to think of himself as a tolerant sort but he'd never forgotten his first conversation with a black man. He'd been six and convinced he'd seen the devil on Hartlepool sea front when a black seaman from a ship in dock had asked him for directions to the King. He'd promptly papped his pants then got a thick ear for his troubles from his granma for 'bein' so rude to that darkie'. He put on a look of polite interest and braced himself.

'I tell you a most amusing tale,' said the doctor.

'Aye, go on then.'

'Northtown are playing Hartlepool in the cup. Before the game Mr Barry says "I beat this lot on my own, what do you say eh?" The fellows laugh and say "yes you must do this". So, he takes the field and they listen to the game on the wireless in the dressing room. After ten minutes Northtown go one up. "Oh," say the men, "it is just as Barry said" and turn to other things. Then as the game comes to a close they switch it back on just as Hampson scores an equaliser with the last kick of the game, then Barry comes in most upset; he has let everyone down, is full of remorse, what a bad thing he has done. "It is fine," they tell him. "You have held them to a draw all by yourself, you are still a fine fellow". "It is not that," he says, "I was sent off after twenty minutes".'

After a pause Dougie burst out laughing and Dr Mbargo joined him. 'You must tell him he is the hero of the hour,' he said then ambled off chuckling, leaving Dougie struggling to remember Clogger Milton ever coming out with stuff like that when they'd been at Middlesbrough together.

For a time while they waited for Ambrose, Barry and Shirley had been joined by an older man in charge of a baby who'd taken one look at Barry and grizzled for the rest of its time with them. They were relieved when a younger woman came in and told the older man 'there's nowt they can do'. After they'd gone Barry told Shirley that he loved her and had never met a girl like her before. After making due allowance for his bang on the head and the chemicals slugging it out in his system, she believed that he probably meant it. 'I love you too Barry,' she said and felt she probably meant it to. She was beginning to see more of the aspiring probation officer alongside the Greek God. It was a potent brew and she'd got the taste. They held hands in the quiet till Ambrose put his duck's arse round the door. On the way home Barry told himself that all he needed was love.

CHAPTER THIRTEEN

JUST WILD ABOUT BARRY

Harold was still dozing when he heard Shirley's voice fading on a closing door, urging Barry to get some sleep. It soon re-opened then Shirley went downstairs. He waited five minutes before joining her in the small front room where she was sketching. The room smelt of fresh cigarette smoke and Shirley. 'Hi Harry,' she said.

'Hi. Lot of excitement for one day, eh? How's Barry?'

She laughed softly through her nose and frowned at something she'd put down on her pad. 'He'll be all right, I need to look in on him every so often but the hospital thinks Barry'll be fine. We went to see Mr Burleson while we were there – Dougie and Mrs B were at the hospital as well. He's not very well you know, there might be permanent damage.'

Harold didn't want to think about this and asked Shirley to show him what she was drawing. It was an impression of a bandaged man in a bed trying to listen to another man viewed from behind leaning in and towards him. Although the man in the bed was clearly unwell and looked distracted, he was also taking in some of what was being said. The jacket and hair signified that the man was Barry so the patient must be Mr Burleson. She explained about the visit and how helpful Barry had been, unlike Dougie: 'Poor chap, couldn't say the right thing to Anita, put off by the doctors. I thought at one point he was going to shout at Mr Burleson.'

'Dougie went to see him?'

'Yes, with Anita – didn't matter, I don't think he knew who they were. Barry made him smile though.'

'Shirley, I've been thinking.'

'Yes?'

'Should we get our heater checked, only – you know?'

'I'm sure we're quite safe Harold,' she said and propped her picture on the mantelpiece. He'd known that she had a real talent but could see it more clearly when her work was sparer and more direct.

'Nobody could take a photograph like that,' he said. Shirley didn't respond directly and continued looking at the drawing before she asked him why not. 'It wouldn't be right – I think people don't want to be made to look foolish or vulnerable.'

'But he didn't know what was happening, and what about my drawing?'

'That's different; you didn't do it at the time and it's just – better really than a photograph would be, maybe a true impression. Also, it could be anyone, it's not forced to be Barry and Mr Burleson. Like I say, they could be anyone.'

'What about the decisive moment though – a drawing couldn't do that?'

'I suppose what I think is should we be snapping them? We talk about shooting pictures – sometimes a camera can feel like a gun.'

'Well,' said Shirley after a pause. 'There are worse things to do to people than take their pictures.'

They sat for a bit longer before Shirley's drawing, then she said, 'Have you ever thought about doing portraits?'

'Formal portraits where people know?'

'Well, yes – what other kind are there?'

Harold was stumped by that but thought he could see what she was getting at. 'I suppose the trick is to make it less intrusive.'

'Or so obvious that it doesn't matter.'

'Like the Victorians, lugging all that kit about the place?'

'Yes, exactly. That's why those portraits look so strong in your face. Julia Marigold Whatsername...?'

'Finlay,' said Harold uncertainly.

'No... Cameron.'

'Julia Margaret Cameron – pictures of Lily.'

'Harry, who are you on about now?'

'Not the Who, pictures of Lily Langtry. And Tennyson and other bearded worthies of yesteryear. I've seen some reproductions at college.'

'Was Lily bearded too?'

'No, but her portrait looked very... stately. Not the kind of thing you'd see done today.'

'Why not? Let's have a go. Fetch your tripod and a sheet and your camera.'

Harold laughed and went off to fetch the props. When he came back Shirley had stretched back the curtains as far as they'd go and unhitched the tatty material serving as a modesty drape. The room was sparsely illuminated by natural light. She was busy with a pile of sun-fried flies on the window ledge and spoke without looking up. 'This is a backstreet photographer's studio in a time of hardship. My name is Lettie and I am a poor girl bound for a new life in far off Americkey and you must catch my likeness, as I may not sit for another. Mark you well the modesty of my station, the gravity of my plight.'

'Right,' said Harold setting up. 'And what is my name?'

'You are, Mr Fisher, a practitioner of the new art which looks fair set to eclipse painting as a mirror to the world. You are also a plain man of few words but who must command the situation.'

'With sitters like you I won't need many words.'

He soon entered into the spirit, placing Lettie on a straight-backed chair in the middle of the room with his tripod set up by the window. After some careful light readings he swept the sheet over his head, tying its corners to the tripod and managed to reproduce the cloaked posture of a Victorian plate-camera man. 'How do you feel my dear, has the modesty of your pose not overcome you?'

'Oh sir, that I cannot say for never have I sat for a gentleman such as yourself. Must I be still before your instrument?'

'Yes, you must compose yourself and follow instruction for the thing to work.'

'Harry you sound very persuasive.'

'Hush Lettie. I require silence for my work.'

'What on Earth's going on here?' said Barry. 'That must have been one bang on the head.'

As Shirley turned to the doorway Harold took her picture, then several more while she talked to Barry, explaining what was going on, that the things he was seeing were real and that he could join in now he was here. 'You can be Mr Penrose, a merchant from Tilbury up on his first visit to the north. Here, sit down and pose for Mr Fisher.' Harold was again able to use the free time before Barry became self-conscious to get some pictures. 'What is your business in the North Country, if I may ask sir?' Harold took another as Mr Penrose thought:

'My journey here concerns coal and cotton.'

Shirley scoffed at this, 'Come on Barry you can do better than that. Cotton's Manchester anyway – be a wandering minstrel or a sporting hero.'

'I've had enough of being a sporting hero, my head still hurts. Harry, will you take one of Shirl and me?'

He adjusted his camera and waited for them to get into position. They looked nice and it made him think about the pictures he'd taken in the greasy spoon on the way to Southend. That must have been around the time when they'd first got together, when Mr Burleson suspected that Barry was after his wife. Or the other way round, now that he'd got to know Barry a bit it was hard for Harold to see him as a seducer from the south. But then it was even harder to see Dougie as the coarse-grained charmer he was. One thing was clear to him though and this was that he was unlikely to get any more lessons in love from Shirley. He came out from behind his curtain to ask Mr Penrose if Lettic would like some tea.

Anita and Dougie had walked all the way from the hospital to her house. 'Everything happens to me,' she said at one point. Dougie had stroked her arm and reflected that it wasn't her as had had her scullery bombed out before coming up with some soothing stuff about 'checking your utilities' when they 'got in'. Her silence was taken as consent that he would be getting across the threshold with her. He reasoned that anything more would be a bonus and felt that this should be the theme. He never minded her silences anyway and assumed this suited her. After about a mile he reached for her hand and she held on till the house was in sight. 'I'll go in first,' she said. 'If anybody asks you've just come to help me sort a few things out.'

He'd half expected some Cuthbert from the *Northern Scene* skulking about the rhododendrons but the only other sign of life was a boy next door playing with a small terrier and his tattered tennis ball. Neither showed much interest in Mrs Burleson or her visitor. Dougie closed the front door behind him and the first thing he noticed was Tom's trilby hat waiting on the hall stand, then a bad smell coming from upstairs. Anita had gone up and was soon wailing. 'Oh Dougie, it's the cat, please do something.' Happy to be occupied he found an old jumper to wrap Tommy and took him out into the back garden from where he discussed the last rites with Anita through an open kitchen window. The dead cat was stiff and decaying but Dougie cradled him and did his best. 'Poor old lad – you'd given him a good life, mind.'

She choked back another sob and said, 'He was a good friend to me was old Tommy. Could you do something for me, pet?'

'Of course.'

'Would you bury him in his favourite part of the garden – just over there by the cat mint?' Dougie made sure he'd got the right spot then was told where to find 'that big shovel'.

The boy from next door had moved into his own back garden where he had been listening carefully across the fence. He went through the details again to make sure he'd got them right.

Dougie felt much better after his digging and went back in for a wash. Anita had made some tea and found a tin of powdered milk. 'Let's go through to the lounge, eh?' she said. They sat quietly for some time, both knew that him being allowed in and allowed to bury the cat was statement enough. And there was better to come when she asked him to remove his shoes. Next door's dog could be heard yapping diffidently, then a door opened and the sound stopped. 'She'll miss Tommy,' said Anita, softly.

'Who's that then?'

'Suzy will – the Jack Russell next door – Tommy used to sun himself on their shed roof deliberately. He got it wrong one time when he thought she'd gone in. Mrs Scully had to come between them.'

Dougie laughed. 'Who's the little lad, then?'

'Oh that's their boy Lawrence – just passed for the Grammar. Tom always said he was destined for the brains trust, used to come round and chatter away when he was out in the garden.'

This poignant vignette caused her to look wistful again and bring home to Dougie that this game was still in its early stages and could go either way yet. 'They're good neighbours, then?

'Yes. Tom and Harry Scully were good pals, did a lot with the Round Table, disabled kiddies and such like. Tom played Father Christmas for them one year, he made it for them – should have seen their faces.' She sipped her tea and looked through her big windows for all the world like a broken Madonna.

Dougie felt like a complete bastard and thought the best thing he could do to complete the effect was to storm round next door and shout at the boy wonder. Instead he offered to check her water tank 'and the rest like'. Anita nodded graciously and he was glad to be up and doing again. Talk of the water tank returned him to thoughts of tragic Tom as had the hat in the hall, the trusty shovel and the finest shortcake biscuits Walter Wilson could provide. Even the blessed cat had managed to suggest the man's mortality as he'd heaped soil over it but was this really any of his fault? Could he be blamed if another man's wife set her cap in his direction or he decided to lay fireworks by Dougie's sink? After a close inspection showed a low level on the central heating but no nasty surprises in the linen cupboard,

207

Dougie turned his attentions to the gas fires, making the most of a 'slow flint' in the back room. Anita was as impressed as ever by his natural command and mannish ways, falling into wifely role by dishing up some Ryvitas and baked beans. These were eaten with more blotchy tea in the smaller room. As she got down a mouthful she delicately licked her lips and Dougie felt himself quicken like he did when she sucked on her cigarettes. 'What are we going to do now?' she said.

He had his answer all worked out, but before he could say anything the chimes bonged by the front door. 'You'd best go,' he said. 'Probably next door calling to see if you're all right.' She left the room and he listened carefully as a serious male voice asked if he might be put in the picture?

She came back with a uniformed policeman Dougie thought he might have seen quelling the masses on match days. He looked very awkward. 'He's come about Tom,' said Anita.

'Oh Christ,' said Dougie. 'I didn't think it would be this soon.' Which caused the young constable to look properly rattled. He asked Dougie where he'd been all evening and asked if he could sit down once he'd heard of his movements. 'Well,' asked Dougie. 'What's this got to do with Mr Burleson?'

'You tell me,' he said. 'When did you last speak to him?'

'It would be about half six at the General, not that we had much to say anyway how is he?'

Anita had become tearful again and beseeched the lad, who looked uncomfortable, to tell her if 'my husband' was all right?

'Yes, yes – well I mean he's no different. I called at the hospital and saw for myself.'

'So what are you doing here upsetting his wife?' put in Dougie, shamelessly.

'Well we must follow up any information leading us to suspect wrongdoing.' This time Dougie blanched and found an interesting spot on the carpet. 'To be plain madam, we've received information telling of diggings in your garden and an old friend who'd made you happy being laid to rest in the twilight. I have to ask you these questions – can you account for this tale?'

Dougie found his second wind. 'I can account for its whiskers and paws as well if you like. Was this old friend called Tommy by any chance?'

'Yes,' said the policeman. 'But it clearly wasn't Mr Burleson.'

'No it was his old moggy Tommy the second. I can dig him back up for you if you want.'

Anita spoke first by offering the young policeman a cup of tea and guessing correctly his source. He seemed relieved and joined them for a seemly chat now that the matter had been cleared up. 'That Barry Hutchinson's a character, isn't he?' he said to Dougie.

'Oh he's that all right, no telling where he'll turn up next.'

'Will he stay at the club?'

'We hope so,' said Anita.

'I should imagine he'll be offered a contract for next season,' said Dougie. 'I think he's found the north quite exciting.'

'Aye,' said the policeman. 'Like Tranmere's goalkeeper.'

'I'm sure that was all another misunderstanding,' said Anita stiffly. 'The man's no more than a lout striking Barry like that.'

Dougie and the policeman shared a knowing look, then he took his leave to call next door and reassure the concerned neighbours. 'She's a good sort really is Batty,' said Anita of the lad's mother.

'Batty?'

'Yes, known as Batty Bainbridge as long as anyone could remember, now she's Batty Scully. Always had an imagination, probably where little Lawrence gets his brains from.'

'Training doesn't start for a bit yet'

'This new stuff's better than Vim, where's it from?'

Eunice looked at the plain cardboard box. 'Kenneth got hold of a job lot from his brother – works up at ICI – reckons when they've got it right it'll shift youknowwhat off a shovel then Vim'll be yesterday's powder of choice for the busy housewife. Mind, for the time being he recommends use with rubber gloves only and get some ventilation while I remember.' She went to open the boot-room door while Reenie went about sifting socks and shin-pads. Her friend joined her and they worked together in silence. Random details came through to them as people moved in and out of earshot; Mr Mullins was heard to say that a sound keeper would weather many a storm and Mrs Robson ask how. This made them smile, then Bob Guthrie poked his sad clowns face round the door. 'What are you at Bob?' asked Eunice. 'Pre-season training doesn't start till next week.'

'I know. I got bored at home, I want to get cracking. Anyone else been in?' Reenie shook her head and he wandered off.

'Wants to mark his card for next season more like,' she said. 'Dot Robson told me they're paying him non-contract because they think he'll struggle and want to see how he shapes up.'

'I reckon they could be right,' said Eumice. 'They'll need to find winning ways directly, there's a much tighter margin for error in this league. There's some big clubs in there next season. You know Rotherham came down and then there's Port Vale and Oxford – we're in with the big boys now, and another thing, there'll be no time for last seasons funny business. Douglas'll have to get things straight and I'm not just talking about his back kitchen. Is he still putting up at yours, Reen?'

'I've barely seen him for weeks now. Haven't you heard the latest?'

CHAPTER FOURTEEN
LIKE A NORTHTOWN COWBOY

Two middle-aged men dance together in a spacious sitting room. Holding each other chastely they shuffle about the carpet to the narcotic swoon of Al Bowly and his band singing *I'll Never be the Same*. The woman in the doorway watches them as the taller of the two catches his reflection in a mirror as they came to a stop by the fireplace. There was no recognition, no returning glance of affirmation, just the fuddled opacity he showed most things now. Dougie caught Anita's pained expression and moved Tom gently to one of the chairs where he sat back quietly as the other two began to talk again.

'I wish you wouldn't make me do that,' said Dougie as the ill-starred crooner, also blown up, but by a direct hit on his hotel by the Luftwaffe, began to sing *The Best Things in Life Are Free*.

'He likes it... and I can't dance with him anymore, can I?'

'I suppose not, but how do you know he likes it? I could just as easily stick him in the garden for a chat with the birdies that sing. It's all the same to him, you know.'

'Is it?'

'Well by my reckoning it is. The other day I told him Northtown had won the European Cup – didn't bat an eyelid.'

'Yes well, soon he might not be able to do that and you know I don't like you teasing him.'

Dougie gave her a despairing look. 'Isn't that just what we're doing?'

'Look, we both know it won't be for long. They reckon in six months he'll need nursing care, it's best he stays here till then. God knows I feel bad enough about it.'

'Well that coloured fellow seems to know his stuff, it's marvelous how he can get through to Tom.' They both looked at the figure in the chair who sat slack-jawed and bereft, lost to sense and the world. Anita started to fill up and shouted at Dougie that it was time for Tom's run. 'Then at least he'll sleep, the poor soul.'

Reenie put down the shin pad she'd been scrubbing and suggested a cup of tea. Eunice put the kettle on while her friend piled up the remaining 'clobber' then, as privacy was required and the noxious vapours had dispersed, she closed the door again and brought Eunice up to date. 'You know that night there was that to-do about them burying Tom Burleson in his back garden..?'

'What a story, eh? As if they'd do a trick like that – it was Batty Scully got it all round her neck, wasn't it?'

'Aye, all thanks to little Lord Snooty earwiging over the fence.'

'Little pitchers,' said Eunice.

This stopped Reenie in full flow. 'Come again?'

'Have big ears.'

'Aye, anyway – that was all sorted out to everyone's satisfaction and Douglas was so helpful and commanding that it brought the lovers together.'

'How masterful do you need to be burying a dead cat? She's easily impressed, is that one.'

'No, it was more the whole thing; the young bobby coming round, things to be seen to, a man's hand on the tiller, our Dougie at his best. Apparently, and all this is from Dot by way of Dulcie Dorman so it's the goods, Anita knew for certain that night.'

'Knew what? That Dougie was a dab hand with a shovel when there's cats to be dug in to the borders, besides I thought they'd let Tom out – discharged him like. Sent him home.'

'They have.' Reenie let the information sink in.

Eunice replaced her cup in its saucer. 'It'll be one of these menageries for three. She'll have some clearing up to do after two of them.'

'What?'

'I heard about it on the wireless the other night. It's where a fellow spreads himself between two women, or vice versa.'

Reenie seemed put out by Eunice's reaction. 'Look, it's nothing like you seem to be suggesting – but it's still a proper turn-up for the books, don't you think?' Eunice picked up her cup and looked at her friend who went on with her story. 'They've moved in together, officially Dougie's there to help mind Tom and then only till his house is set to rights, but in a house that size there's plenty of room for manoeuvres, after dark as well. With Tom being three parts cracked who's to say what goes on?'

'Hmm,' said Eunice. 'And what do they reckon to Tom Burleson then?'

'Well, I've heard he'll make some sort of physical recovery – which is where our man of the moment comes in with his physio – but the damage up top is bad and can only get worse.

He may need to go away at some point, they say he's like a great baby.'

'How awful. Who's told you this like?'

'Mrs Suggett from down Olympic Street. Says she's seen Dougie out coaching him in Green Park. Takes him for an ice cream afterwards at Signor Jaconellis.'

'Well,' said Eunice. 'I've heard some things now. Has Dougie spoken to you?'

'I don't see that much of him these days now that he's got his hands full with both Burlesons, as you might say; but I think he's a changed man, 'specially since he made things up with his Robert. Last time I spoke to him was last week, he came round wanting to know where that soft lad with the camera lived.'

'What did he want him for?'

'A picture he wanted taking of the three of them round at Lady B's.'

'Haway man, this gets dafter.'

'No listen, he wanted one blown up to stick by Mr Burleson's bed so that when he woke up he'd know where he was and what was what.'

'And whose bright idea was that, then?'

'This African chap at the hospital. Dougie swears by him.'

'I can believe that. Roll on the new season and things can get back to normal round here.'

As Eunice spoke other unhistoric acts were moving through time at the Northtown Stadium. Mrs Robson climbed the stairs to see what colour would be required in a refurbished directors' suite, Mr Mullins telephoned his counterpart at Tranmere to inquire about the availability of his goalkeeper and Kenneth the groundsman dismantled his white liner.

And Dougie led Tom through three gentle circuits of the bottom end of Green Park. He brought them to rest on the seat where Shirley had begun her seduction of Harold. Tom panted for a bit like an old retriever who would never catch rabbits again, then gave Dougie his vacant grin. Dougie couldn't help himself, 'Well Mr Barmpot what's it to be – ice cream, nice glass of sherry, your wife back?'

Tom chuckled and nodded at a blackbird, Dougie felt rotten but comforted himself that he was at least paying for his pleasures and that Tom was sleeping more these days. In some ways he almost envied him. As they got up to go Tom faltered and, as Dougie braced himself, he fell forward into his arms. He thought he heard a sudden click from somewhere but when he looked he could only see the blackbird and hear another one chipping out of view. He steadied his charge and they walked off up the hill.

Anita was in the garden pouring out tea while another blackbird darted about the borders. Tom had 'gone down' for his rest which would probably take up the rest of his day and Dougie was tucking into tomato sandwiches. Anita had thought of something. 'It's like that song they put on the radio the other day.'

It was worse than trying to explain the offside law to Bob Guthrie. 'Come again pet?'

'*I'm a Linesman for the County* – it could be your song Dougie only you weren't still on the line that day, were you?'

He felt his hackles rising. 'How do you mean 'Nita?'

She began to sing, quite loudly he thought. 'And I need you more than want you, and I want you for all time... and you're still on the line... du du der der du d du d du de du du...'

215

He'd forgotten that women sang. 'Yes, yes all very nice I'm sure, but let's forget all about that carry-on.'

'Dougie pet, I've often wondered, was it me you were thinking about that day?'

'Of course it was.' And maybe it had been, who was he to know? 'Who sings this song then, it's not Stockport County they're on about is it?'

'I don't think so. It's Glen Campbell, I think I'll buy it.'

'It's not him that plays for Dundee is it? He's one to be singing songs. They had him on trial at Middlesborough – he was drunk at training, I'd not pay him in washers. When I was a young player just making my way in...'

'It can't be him, this chap's American, a country boy with his hair in a fringe, apparently.'

'Well he's got a Jock's name anyway and Jim Baxter's hair's down his collar.'

'Yes but Raymond Baxter has a Scottish name and he sounds like Prince Phillip. Got a lovely speaking voice.'

'Don't let's get on to him, he'd sing 'The Desert Song' for you.'

'He's Greek.'

'Aye well. Good footballers mind, would beat Scotland I'd say.'

'I thought Scotland were good. Didn't they beat England at Wembley?'

'Only because Billy Bremner crippled Ray Wilson, dirty little beggar. Young Atkinson'll learn some bad ways when he goes down there.'

'Is Bremner the one who sells paint?'

'No pet, you're thinking of Paul Madeley. I'll set him on with my kitchen when it's ready, eh?'

Dougie had enjoyed their playful chat, despite Anita bringing all that up again, but she was the only person in the world he would take it from. He had begun to look ahead now anyway, to how their life together might be. He could experiment with a fringe, drink rum and coke just like 'Slim Jim' Baxter had done at last year's Sportsman's dinner, Robbie and his young lady could stay over for the weekend once Tom was out of the picture, but that was thinking too far into the future. Were these things he wanted more than needed? He let the reverie take root as Anita tended Tommy's memorial, picturing a ten-gallon life not far from Cactusville where Desperate Dan lived forever in Robbie's old copies of *The Dandy*. Many a queer notion seemed possible just then as his woman watered the grave of a dead cat and her brain-damaged husband slumbered a medicated afternoon away above them, a cuckolded simpleton. Why not frame the happier life in a Wild West town, a fantastic place with sage brush, gas mains and a town council, Red Indians, meat pies and a football team? Barry Hutch would be the whisky-drinking card sharp, Bob Guthrie would run the store and go to church Sundays where Reenie Hardwick led the singing. A harmonious place where things worked out. Big Bill Thompson would be out of harm's way up on Boot Hill. Each evening the men would meet to discuss the best way to live. He made himself more comfortable in the green deckchair while upstairs Tom turned peacefully losing himself further.

Anita went inside and picked up the day's *Northern Scene*. A new swimming baths was planned for the town, Shildon's May Queen day would be photographed exclusively by "local lensman" Harold Hare and the cuckoos had come back to Newton Aycliffe.

Northtown Exposure